PACIFIC HOPE

S.L. BOLIN

THE HOPE WITHIN

DISCLAIMER

This is a work of fiction. Names, characters, places, and incidents are either products of the author's imagination, or if real, are used fictitiously.

DEDICATION

This book is dedicated to my grandmother, *Christina Potter* grandmother, *Sharon Bolin,* grandfather, *David Treon* and great-grandmother, *Wilma Earls.*

In memory of those killed during the attacks on December 7th, 1941, at Pearl Harbor, including 68-civilians and throughout the second World War.

PROLOGUE

Thomas glared anxiously through the descending window seat glass as the Hawaiian sunset grew fuller in color by the second. Even though it had been over three years, 1,500 days, and millions of minutes since he saw the O'ahu sky in the evening, it seemed brighter than he remembered. The jolt of landing shook Thomas out of his daydream.

Not only had it been years since he'd seen that beautiful Hawaiian sky, but it had been just as long since he saw the most gorgeous woman. Through dogfights over the Pacific, lonely nights on patrols, and hopeless duels with hell, all Thomas could think about was the first time he laid eyes on Kawai and seeing her face just one more time. Thoughts of their life together and all he had endured since last seeing her raced through his mind.

CHAPTER 1

The date was December 5th, 1941, and neither Thomas nor his right-hand man, Lance Jones, knew what kind of nightmare would precede them over the next 48-hours. All they could think about was another night on the town.

It was going bar-to-bar for Lance and talking to as many women as he could fit into his few hours away from training. Whether it was a nurse from just across the base or a local O'ahu *wahine,* he attempted various pick-up lines in-between training sessions that he planned to use the following Friday and Saturday night. On the other hand, Thomas had his eyes set on one girl. THE girl.

Kawai Mehelona was THE girl. Born and raised on the Island of O'ahu, Kawai worked day and night at her family's theater, which sat just miles outside Wheeler Airfield, where Thomas spent most of his time training. From the time Kawai could walk and talk, her family involved her with the family business. Whether cleaning restrooms, selling tickets or making popcorn, she did it all. Into adulthood, Kawai had no time for boys or friends. For more than fifteen years, whenever she wasn't in school, Kawai worked to survive, from sunrise to sunset.

Even thousands of miles away from the heart of Black Tuesday, The Great Depression could be felt in every corner of Hawaii, and the Mehelona family was no different. Mr. and Mrs. Mehelona ensured their daughter was prepared to help them through the most significant economic collapse the islands had ever seen.

Local soldiers and nurses were all that kept the O'ahu Golden Era Theater alive during the economic collapse, which made Kawai curious about American culture. Though she looked far different than the pale, blond-haired women with red lips that would come each weekend, American pilots were all she knew, and Kawai always dreamed about the possibility of romance with a Fly Boy.

Thomas hadn't planned how he would win Kawai over and convince her that he wasn't just another pilot looking for something fast; because every time he tried, all he could think about was how beautiful she was. He could train for hours, one mistake away from certain death, and not blink an eye, but the thought of Kawai made his heartbeat faster than any loop or barrel roll. Her skin was smooth and warm, touched by every sunset since her birth twenty-one years before. She had long, stout, curly hair that resembled nothing like Thomas had ever seen before. He was star-struck by her eyes that put the Pocono autumn leaves from his childhood to shame and a smile more evident than the white star on the wing of his Curtiss P-40.

Few things in Thomas's life made him feel the way Kawai did, without ever talking to her. It felt like his first hit in Little League when girls didn't matter or the Navy finally giving him his wings after two years of training. Kawai represented freedom, home, and peace that he yearned to explore.

As Thomas sat and waited for Lance to finish getting ready for their night out, he realized he had been searching for these feelings since leaving his sleepy hometown in Pennsylvania. Growing up, and even since joining the Navy, it has been all about work and doing what he had to do to survive. Like Kawai's childhood at the theater, at Thomas's family farm, the thought of starvation and poverty was around every corner, which left little room for excitement.

Though the anxiety of a pending war with a faceless enemy plagued Thomas's mind, seeing Kawai brought happiness and gave him something to shoot for outside of his cockpit. Meeting and talking to women wasn't hard for Lance. He had a new girl every night, and that was by design. For Thomas, meeting his one and only was his sole focus with a woman, if there was one at all.

"We've gone to this place nearly every weekend for God knows how many months, and you haven't said two words to her," Lance said. "What makes you think this will be any different?"

"Tonight's the night," Thomas responded, running his fingers through his hair. "There's just something about tonight; maybe it's the direction of the *waves, wind, sun,* something, I just know. Besides, who knows how many more chances I will get before we're shipped off somewhere else."

"Just stay close to me; I haven't looked this good in weeks," Lance said with a laugh and punch to Thomas's arm as the two approached the theater entrance. "If you're lucky, she'll talk to you long enough to get to me; use that time wisely."

Lance had a way of irritating and pushing away the other pilots in the squadron, but Thomas didn't mind it. He knew that once you put Lance in a plane, and a sticky situation, that attitude which many viewed as too cocky and confident, would be a best-case scenario for the two of them to get through the battle alive. You had to be sure of yourself in the air and make split-second decisions without thought. It was the difference between life and death.

Some had laid-back confidence, did their thinking and worrying on the ground, so when they fired the engine on the P-40, their fear had already been dealt with. Thomas was that kind of man and pilot: think in private, perform without doubt in the air and on the ground. On the other hand, Lance dealt with his fear and the situation around him without acknowledging it. Life was a game to Lance, inside the cockpit and outside of it, especially with the ladies.

As the two approached the Golden Era entrance, Thomas began to pressure himself. He knew that even though those around him played off the advancements of Hilter's Army in Europe and the unpredictability of the Japanese Empire, America would be at war eventually. Those worries, coupled with the fact that he was sure other sailors or pilots, not to mention locals that Kawai had grown up with, would swoop in and sweep her off her feet before he could, put Thomas on pins-and-needles.

Lance made quick work of purchasing his ticket and making a beeline for a nurse that had left him with a side-eye the weekend before. Even for a man who took orders for a living, he remained persistent with the ladies.

"You go ahead," Thomas said, as Lance turned towards him.

"Thomas, we've been through this too many times," Lance responded. "You're talking to her, tonight."

"I will, just give me a minute," Thomas demanded; waving and pointing. "Go."

When he joined the Navy in February of '39, Thomas put the dream of meeting the love of his life in passing and everything else for the rest of his life, playing background to the bond between him and that shotgun romance, to rest. There was no time or motivation. Kawai or someone like her wasn't even a blip on his radar. The military was training him for war.

Since Black Tuesday and the passing of his grandparents, who were in love until their last breath, the Metic household was focused on one thing: survival. His parents no longer loved each other but lived under the same roof, out of obligation, nothing more. Siblings had been married, divorced, and in one case, widowed before thirty. The whirlwind romance his grandparents had instilled in him as a young boy, with their picturesque portrayal of love, had been overshadowed by a decade of darkness, negativity, and depression, years before he put on the uniform or saw Kawai's unforgettable eyes.

During his first year of service, Thomas was micro-focused, poised to make his worthless drunk of a father proud. He never wrote home, went out, or even opened a book. It was head down, studying, training, and resting for the next day around the clock. Going out didn't interest Thomas, as this was the first time he could remember where he had a roof over his head and a clear path to success. Women, getting drunk with his peers and waking up just to not remember what had happened, didn't interest him one bit. Then fate stepped in, and he was stationed at Pearl Harbor.

The first time he was introduced to Lance, a pilot, who had been stationed at Pearl and trained through Wheeler Airfield for a few months before Thomas arrived, he was talking about a girl. Lance didn't take the time to introduce himself before asking Thomas's opinion on his outfit for the evening. The energy in Hawaii was far more laid back and calm than Thomas had ever experienced since enlisting.

Months went by without adjustment, Thomas kept to the same daily routine: up before dawn, first one in, last one to leave, and his uniform in pristine shape every hour in-between. The number-one rule he stuck by during this time was no alcohol under any circumstances. Thomas had watched his dad drink his way out of a marriage and career while letting years be taken off his life. Following in those footsteps wasn't an option.

Lance worked around the clock to convince Thomas to go out with him during his weekend shenanigans; offering to train harder, wake up with him, study new tactics, and even drink less himself. Lance promised to change his attitude in the sky, be less cocky and more consistent, though he never came through, making sure to call himself "L-Ace," whenever the opportunity arose. Day-after-day, weekend-after-weekend, the two engaged in the same conversation.

"Tom, we're going out to see a show tonight. It's time you had a night away from this base, room, and your bed," Lance demanded.

"It's the weekend, time to rest and re-charge," Thomas replied. "When Hitler comes knocking, I'll be well-rested and ready to fight. You'll be stumbling over bottles and putting your boots on the wrong feet."

"When Hitler comes knocking, hell will be so frozen over that his crummy little hands won't even be able to shave that god-awful mustache," Lance said with a chuckle. "One night, Tommy, just give me one night on the town."

"What is there to gain?" Thomas asked with frustration. "Is going out, talking to a nurse who looks and acts the same as the next ten women beside her going to help me prepare for anything?"

"No," Lance replied as he started going through Thomas's shirts, looking for something for him to wear. "It's not going to help that; it's going to take your mind off war, which for one, we prepare every day for, and two, we're never going to be in. Fun Tom, *fun*, something you need more than sleep or another study session."

"I don't know, man. Get out of my stuff," Thomas said as he walked towards Lance, pulling the closet door shut. "There will be plenty of fun to be had once this war is over; I'll celebrate then."

"Put this on and let's go," Lance demanded as he grabbed a white button-up shirt and handed it to Thomas. "One night, and if you don't enjoy yourself, I won't bring it up again."

"I'm not drinking. Hey, *I'm not drinking*," Thomas stated, grabbing Lance's arm as he started to walk away.

"You don't have to," Lance replied as he jerked his arm away, giving Thomas a gentle shove. "Now, let's go."

Thomas gave in and went with Lance to the theater even with doubt in his mind and annoyance on a bitten tongue. As the two made their way into the theater, Lance already had a gal waiting for Thomas, which was weeks in the planning. Lance made sure that his date for the evening had a friend for Thomas, just in case he decided that night was the one he'd break out of his shell and go out.

Though Thomas was surprised and appreciative that his best new pal had set him up, many times, there was a slight issue that developed while the two bought their tickets for the picture show.

"This isn't gonna work," Thomas said with a smirk as he pointed towards the two women waiting for himself and Lance.

"And why is that? Maria is obsessed with you already; I'm not sure why, but she is," Lance asked with a frustrated look. "Also, why are you smiling like that? Do you understand how hard this was to put together?"

"Look, calm down and hear me out," Thomas said with his arms held out in front of him in a placating manner. "That woman is the most beautiful human being I have ever seen in my life. She is out of this world. You've been to Pennsylvania; have you seen anything like her? She is one of a kind, and I have to figure out what is behind that perfect smile."

"Then let's go talk to her," Lance demanded, pulling Thomas by the arm. "You make no damn sense sometimes. What are you waiting for?"

"Not Maria, you twit, her," Thomas explained as he ripped his arm away from Lance and pointed in Kawai's direction. "She's perfect."

"Ah. I see," Lance said with a smile. "Well, let's just get through tonight, and then you can come back and talk to her tomorrow."

"Not a chance," Thomas replied as he backed away from Lance and turned towards the exit. "A girl like that you must plan for. I need to go back to base and think about this. Think about what to say, how to approach her and a whole list of other things."

"You're serious?" Lance asked with his hands up.

"As the Luftwaffe," Thomas said as he turned and left the theater.

With the sunset painting a promising foreground, Thomas felt a sense of fullness and freedom he had not experienced since those evenings sitting on the front porch with his grandparents he cherished so much. There was something to look forward to and something to lift the pressure of war preparation from his shoulders. Thomas had only looked into the woman's eyes once, and he was already on cloud nine. The world around him seemed so small for those few seconds, and the worrying that plagued his mind faded away. He noticed the stars forming behind the sunset for the first time since he set foot on the island and looked forward to the sunrise in a way he never had. Tomorrow was a new kind of challenge.

Thomas developed tactics for a living, but this challenge required a whole new set of preparation. He set off on a new adventure, developing ways to make their first conversation special, not just a moment in passing. Nights lying awake were spent wondering if he would ever have the guts or confidence to go through with his plans. If the pain left from his parents' failed relationship would alter his ability to try for a love himself like they had prior in his life.

For Thomas, many relationships had fallen apart one they'd reached long-term commitment. Though he wasn't sure why that was the case, many signs, he realized, pointed towards his rough teenage years, where his parents went through poverty, unfaithfulness, and times of verbal and physical abuse, but stayed together because it was the more affordable thing to do. Thomas tried to put that behind him and give his own love life a try through high school and even a few dates during various moments in the service.

Images and memories of his dad's drunken hand flying across his mother's unfaithful but undeserving face had him counting down the days until he could sign-up for the Navy. It was a laser-focused lifestyle, where the pain of the past was pushed deeper into his soul than his foot on the pavement when training. Love was nowhere to be found. When it was, hope, confidence, and the fearlessness he had behind his goggles, didn't exist with them off and the possibility of forever staring him in the face.

Nights of sitting awake, thinking about the woman's perfect smile and autumn eyes, became frequent. How he would overcome his demons and the doubt from the past to speak to her weighed heavy on his mind. Those nights grew tiring, and the frustration of doubt pushed Thomas towards her instead of away from her, which was a welcomed sign. Thomas wanted to take a chance, just this once; if it didn't work out, he'd go back to his laser-focused lifestyle with no regrets. All he needed was Lance on-his-six, an O'ahu sunset for good spirits, and just a pinch of luck.

After a few moments outside in the fresh Hawaiian air, Thomas gathered himself enough to make his move. Thomas was relieved Kawai was working the concession stand and not the ticket booth, as the theater door swung open. Stuttering his way through small talk, dropping his change, and forgetting his ticket at the counter, Thomas was a show to anyone looking for a laugh.

With Lance nowhere to be found, Thomas decided to head to the bathroom and gain his composure before talking to the woman he had fallen for without ever speaking to. He knew that the best chance he had to talk to her alone, without being rushed or distracted, was after the show began and most had taken their seats.

A prayer to the man upstairs, a splash of water to his face and comb through his slicked-back dark brown hair, and Thomas was as ready as he ever could be. There was nothing between himself and Kawai other than the doubt swirling in the back of his mind. All he could do was wait as the last few guests grabbed their food and proceeded to the show.

With only a mother and her child before it was his turn to talk to her, look into those gorgeous eyes and experience her signature smile up close, Thomas's plan began to fall apart. He was flanked from the right by an enemy that could have given the Axis powers a run for their money and dropped a bomb on everything he had spent days planning. Kawai's father approached the counter to relieve his daughter from her duties and send her off to break. As Mr. Mehelona started to speak, the family in front of Thomas moved aside. He took that as a sign from God that now was the time to throw a Hail Mary.

This was it, make his move now or watch another pilot sweep her off to forever. Act or watch the theater from his cockpit until Uncle Sam decided to ship him off to another island or a destroyer in the middle of the ocean. He may leave Hawaii tomorrow for a training mission and never return, which meant right now would be the first step to the rest of his life, one way or another. There was no time for regrets, second thoughts, or anxious feelings. "Interrupt him," Thomas thought. "Now or never."

"Excuse me miss, I've been watching you for a while," Thomas said sternly as Kawai began to peal her greasy apron off and hand it to her father. "I mean, I've noticed you and have been trying to come up with the words to come and introduce myself."

"Son, those are not the words you were looking for," Mr. Mehelona said with a chuckle as he ushered his daughter away. "We have work to do; enjoy the show."

Thomas watched as the woman who held so much mystery walked away, turning her head to him with a smile and a wave brushed away by her father. He couldn't fathom what had happened. How could it all go wrong that fast? She was the one, and he knew deep down she was. From the time he was a boy, his grandfather and grandmother would tell stories about how they met for hours on the front porch. It was love at first sight, and from that moment on, nothing else mattered. Making a living, friends and even family came second to the love they formed and the life they built together. Every win was sweeter, loss more manageable, and moment cherished just a bit longer than before.

CHAPTER 2

Thomas entered through the theater door with the opening credits of *Dive Bomber* playing in the foreground. He quickly found a seat, as far away from Lance and his date as possible, the pit in his stomach grew larger. Disappointment, sadness, and regret filled Thomas's mind and body. All sorts of negative thoughts ran through his head. After weeks of planning, he couldn't believe the moment came and went, without even an ounce of success.

Lance could have a different woman every single weekend, a new nurse to take out and not think twice about it. Thomas asked himself why he couldn't be more like Lance, and it didn't just stop with women. Of course, thoughts of why he couldn't just settle for a nurse or bounce from woman to woman like Lance entered his mind, but the idea ran much more profound.

Why couldn't he live as freely as Lance does? Why did he have to study so hard instead of just getting into the cockpit, firing the engine, and flying the damn airplane? Why, instead of the hundreds of available and enthusiastic women did Thomas have to chase the shy, sheltered Hawaiian girl?

Thomas knew nothing about Hawaiian culture, and although he had been through his fair share of struggle, there was no way of relating to what Kawai or her family went through on a daily basis. She must think he's just another arrogant American, coming onto her land without any appreciation for the Hawaiian people forced to become welcoming hosts. If that wasn't the case, she surely wouldn't be impressed by the way Thomas started their first conversation.

Close to an hour passed, with Errol Flynn and Alexis Smith putting on a memorable show on the big screen. Only, Thomas's mind was everywhere but following the storyline. He couldn't care less about the show or snacks he bought. If it wasn't Kawai or how much he messed up with her, on his mind, it was his childhood and what possibly could have made him put so much pressure on every single day and every single interaction with someone. If Thomas had even the slightest passion for something, he blocked out the rest of the world and dove headfirst into it, setting himself up for disappointment.

Thomas's mind wandered back to that damp, weathered front porch, listening to his two favorite people recite a romance story for the ages. In the twenty-one years he'd been alive, his grandparents were the only example of true, everlasting love he had to base his own experiences on. They were everything a Hollywood story could ask for. Love at first sight, a baby boy first, a girl second, pets, a farm, and financial freedom. Plenty of time for memory-making and no time for worrying about what tomorrow may bring. The two passed away weeks from each other, a few months shy of Black Tuesday, and years before the Metic family turned from the American Dream to a Pocono Mountain Horror Film.

With the final few minutes of the film wrapping up in the distance, Thomas wondered if he would end up alone, with no story to tell. A tale he wouldn't want to tell like his parents, or maybe, just maybe, someone would come along, and he'd have a fairytale-like his grandparents. As Thomas tried to convince himself of positivity and reassurance of his age, places in the world he would go, and years of potential love ahead, he caught an unbelievable sight from the corner of his misty eye.

"Aloha," Kawai said as she approached Thomas with the brightest smile he had ever seen. "Is this seat taken?"

"No, no, it's all yours," Thomas struggled to respond with a nervous smile.

"Thank you, sorry about my father," Kawai apologized as she brushed Thomas's hand with hers. "He can be very protective, especially towards American men who try to talk to me."

"Not all of us are the same," Thomas assured. "I hadn't thought about women for years until the first time I saw you, and something inside me changed. I had to get to know you, and I ruined my chance."

"You didn't ruin your chance," Kawai said as she stood up to walk away. "You can't be nervous all the time or have so much doubt; life is too short. Meet me around back in fifteen minutes."

Thomas didn't know what was harder to believe as he sat in awe; Kawai walking back into his life with a gifted second chance or that his heart hadn't stopped yet with how fast it was beating. He couldn't believe what had happened, and without letting himself overthink the situation like he always did, Thomas shot up, gathered his things, and finally made his way out of the emptied theater.

"Damn man, I didn't even see you in there," Lance said as Thomas hurried past without stopping. "Wait-up, how did things go with the woman at the counter?"

"Can't talk," Thomas said. "I'll see you back at base later, don't wait for me."

There was no time to waste. Thomas quickly stopped by the bathroom to make sure he was presentable. With the butterflies filling his stomach, he was out the door, waiting on the woman he would wait an eternity for if he had to. As Kawai approached him, she appeared exhausted from a day's work, but still as beautiful as ever. Thomas was amazed that Kawai seemed to get more gorgeous each time he saw her. The curls bouncing on her shoulders were just a touch more defined and her smile shined in the moonlit sky brighter than any streetlight.

The two passed through backyards, business parking lots, and backroads to avoid being seen by anyone who would relay the message to Kawai's dad that she was out past dark with an American pilot en route to the beach. Though Thomas spent his day training for war, manhandling a bomb with wings, was nothing compared to the adrenaline he felt running through the O'ahu countryside with the woman of his dreams alongside. The moon was bright but paled in comparison to the perfect bronze glow of Kawai's skin. The universe was the artist, and, on this night, it painted a picture of sandy, blossoming young love under a moonlit Hawaiian sky.

Kawai had called the island home for her entire life, and Thomas had spent the better part of the past year taking in the star-riddled Hawaiian landscape, but as they both walked and talked, neither could compare this night to any they had experienced before. Maybe it was Thomas's grandparents giving him a boost or the spirit of Aloha pushing Kawai to take a chance, but the stars had aligned, and with every passing minute, the two grew closer.

Their conversations covered every subject as they battled the rising tide and windy temperatures. Thomas learned about Kawai's childhood and how her family had dreams in the wine business before prohibition and the Great Depression put all hopes to bed. She spoke about her father's challenges running their theater to a rowdy American Military customer base and how he put a smile on his face, creating a family environment even though their people upended his.

Thomas had no clue about Americans taking over Hawaiian land for their benefit, with little care for the natives just trying to get by on their homeland. Stories of the horror Kawai's ancestors faced just years before her birth left Thomas speechless. Kawai told him about Princess Ka'iulani and the hope she brought to young Hawaiian girls all over the Island, and the impact she left behind after only 23-years of life.

Thomas had never taken the time to learn about the history of the land he trained on and the skies he flew through. While sitting with Kawai in her native sand, he realized that he was a visitor, a guest in a house that wasn't his nor his country's. Even with the cards the Mehelona family had been dealt by the United States government and the limited opportunities provided by the times they all lived in, her positivity blew Thomas away. Kawai had dreams, aspirations which most could not begin to imagine.

"Have you seen the winery that overlooks our theater?" Kawai asked as she stood up with a sense of excitement. "I'm going to buy that building one day, and it's going to be the most beautiful winery in the world. People from all over will travel to taste the wine made by Kawai Mehelona. Paris, Rome, and New York City will all travel to O'ahu. You will see!"

"I believe you," Thomas said with a chuckle as he placed one arm on his knee and the other up to grab Kawai's outstretched hand. "Tell me more."

"Well, since you asked," she said with a huge smile. "When you come inside, there will be a restaurant with the most delicious cheese, a stained wood bar longer than you've ever seen, and paintings of all that make Hawaii unique. All the diverse climates, traditions, and stories from The Kingdom of Hawaii, Princess Ka'iulani, and examples of aloha everywhere you turn."

"Will you save me a seat at the bar on opening night?" Thomas asked as he stood up, with his hand placed firmly in Kawai's.

"If you're lucky," Kawai said as she twirled around, and the two began walking down the beach once more.

Hours passed, and both felt as if they had known each other for years. The outside world mattered very little in those moments, and they wished time could just stop. Anything to feel each first for as long as they could. Whatever they had to do to make those minutes feel like hours and hours like days. The sunrise was their enemy, not Hitler or any Japanese Zero. The thought of war, or any danger, didn't exist. Negative thoughts had no place between them. Even when Thomas began to tell Kawai his life story, she found a way to make him feel hopeful as she had all night.

Kawai did most of the talking as the night aged, but Thomas didn't mind. He fell for her gorgeous voice, contagious personality, and inspiring perspective with every passing conversation. However, when Thomas did talk, he made those few words count, speaking from the heart and leaving nothing unsaid. He wanted Kawai to know who he was and the experiences that had shaped him into the man he had become.

Conversations about his grandparents were lengthy, and the smile he carried through them spoke volumes to Kawai. Evenings on the front porch, lessons each October harvesting the fields, and comedic trips to the ice cream shop were moments Thomas cherished. Stories about his mother and father weren't as long, and Thomas wasn't as passionate. Kawai listened intently as Thomas explained how his parents had run out of love around the same time the rest of the country ran out of money. He pondered if that was a coincidence and Kawai tried to understand how two people could co-exist, without faithfulness, simply because it made cents, not necessarily sense. Though the idea was hard to comprehend, she never cracked, remaining engaged, ready to respond with positivity whenever the opportunity arose.

"I can't imagine going through the things you have," Kawai explained with an encouragingly soft tone, turning toward Thomas and holding both of his hands as the two stopped walking. "It must have been hard, but look at where you are and who you are. You fly fighter planes for the United States Navy but just took the time to care about my people's history. Your mom and dad didn't help you understand love at all, but you talked to me first and were gentle. I've only known you for a few hours and have heard just a fraction of your story, but I am already proud and excited to know more. You've proven that even the roughest of roots can produce the most beautiful and strong trees."

Thomas was speechless, hugging Kawai closely. Never had he heard such words from someone since his grandma. It amazed him that a woman he had never spoken to when he woke earlier that day not only cared enough to say those words to him but realized that's exactly what he needed to hear.

Endless training schedules, lack-lust theater sales, unappreciative guests, and challenging childhoods had taken their toll on Kawai and Thomas, but as the sun started to rise in the east, a few things became evident to them both. No matter the sheltered atmosphere Kawai grew up in, with a family becoming servants to get by and very little room for dreams and aspirations, she kept a smile on her face and hope in her heart. Kawai was the positivity Thomas longed for. Even with her struggles, she gave everything inside her to make sure he knew that he mattered to her and that she cared.

And in return? Thomas listened to Kawai- let her dream, vent, and laugh without interruption or censure. Though it was simple, Kawai felt free with him, away from the direction of her father, the straightforwardness of her mother, and the theater that felt like a prison. A prison where, in her mind, she served those who served their country, on her soil. Even though he was one of those men, Thomas was different. Kawai could be herself around him without worry of judgment or consequence.

With the dawn sunrise peeking through the mountain, the two decided to return home. Even though they had the best night of their lives, there was work to be done. Kawai had to sneak into her house before her parents awoke for the day, hoping to catch a few hours of sleep before heading off to the theater to prep for the busy night ahead. Thomas wasn't so lucky. He was due to report for training at 0700, which was fast approaching, and sleep was nowhere to be found.

Thomas rushed Kawai along, approaching the destination where they would part for the day. He realized that he was rushing to end a night he spent months wishing for. He wished he had a pause button to slow time and savor each moment. Lance had shown up to training often with little to no sleep. If he could do it, Thomas most certainly could; besides, since it was too late to grab any shut-eye, he might as well make each moment count.

"You know how you told me your dream was to own the winery?" Thomas asked as he stopped in his tracks, turning Kawai towards him.

"Yes, that's been my dream for as long as I could understand what wine was," Kawai assured him with a sleepy smile and chuckle. "Why?"

"Well, my dream is to have a huge farm. I don't even care what kind of crops are on it," Thomas said with confidence. "I want to have a wraparound porch, just like my grandparents had, and one day, when I have grandkids of my own, and they're out playing with their toys or having lunch on a Sunday afternoon, I'm going to tell them about my life. I'm going to share every detail about the night I fell for the girl who had the flower behind her ear and the biggest, most beautiful sleepy smile anyone could have. Stories to give them hope, just like she gave me."

Leaving all of her feelings in Thomas's arms crossed Kawai's mind as she stood there speechless, with the Hawaiian sunrise growing by the second. It would have been the easy thing to do... jump into his arms, feel his lips for the first time and confess all of her desires right there, to a man she barely knew. Instead, she settled for a kiss on the cheek and the perfect hug to start a quiet O'ahu morning.

"I'd be the luckiest girl in the world to have a place in your dream," Kawai said, with a grin, as she took Thomas by the hand and started towards a shambled boardwalk.

As they reached a walkway and the sounds of a busy Saturday morning, the dawn of December 6th fell over two people from opposite worlds, sharing a mutual understanding that some could only dream of. The hours of their day passed like decades, as they couldn't wait to start the plans they'd quickly made.

With every exercise and practice maneuver Thomas checked off his agenda, he would catch just a whiff of Kawai's perfume, sending his heart through a tailspin. Through every bag of popcorn Kawai prepared or ticket she punched, the thought of Thomas's passion as he shared his dream of the future kept coming back.

She imagined fitting herself in that dream, like a missing puzzle piece. And the more those thoughts pushed towards a potential reality, the more alive Kawai felt. Butterflies played peek-a-boo in her stomach, racing up and down like the valves on a steam engine.

While the Japanese Empire moved through the weeds, inching towards Battleship Row's doorstep, Kawai and Thomas stared at the clock, waiting for quitting time.

Five o'clock struck, and Thomas rushed to his barracks for a quick change and workout, hoping to clear his mind and focus on what would be a fairytale night with an even more magical woman. He couldn't wait to surprise Kawai with a reservation at the Aloha Sun Winery Restaurant, hoping to hear more about her dreams of running the place and where he may fit into that scenario. Thomas knew everything was set up perfectly. All he had to do was check off his final daily task, shower, and head for Kawai's doorstep.

Growing up with very little, Kawai had dreamt about the day she could wear her favorite Kahala dress and place a Hibiscus behind her ear for a night out with THE man. Before her dream could come to fruition, every event of the day tried to prevent it- having to cover her tasks at the theater, which always ran past their scheduled time, helping an elderly neighbor on the way home, and a second guess in the mirror made her late and left Thomas waiting on the doorstep.

By the time Kawai was ready, Thomas had already persuaded her parents, on his own, that he was a good enough guy to at least grace her presence for the evening. He talked with Mr. and Mrs. Mehelona about their people as if he were one of them, impressing Kawai with his listening skills and commitment to making sure her family knew he didn't view himself as above them in class.

Whether they accepted him as the guy for their daughter or not, it was necessary to Thomas that the Mehelona family understood he wasn't the same as some Americans they had run into at the theater. He wasn't there to take over their land, be a terrible guest or act like he was entitled to special treatment because he wore a uniform and had a painted star on his plane. Thomas most definitely didn't have bad intentions with Kawai, and whatever he had to do to convince her family of that, no matter how long it took, he was going to do.

As Kawai made her way down the stairs and finally into Thomas's sight, she was unlike anything he had laid his eyes on before. Kawai's bright red novelty Kahala halter that her mom wore the night she met Kawai's father made her rich bronze skin glow. Her red lipstick outlined the most gorgeous smile God had ever created. Above Kawai's right ear, a flower made her perfect brown eyes blossom. When Thomas looked into her eyes, it made his heart and voice skip. Kawai represented a new beginning for Thomas. Her eyes reminded him of a free-flowing Pocono leaf, ending a season in God's sky by floating to the surface of the ocean and starting again.

With his stare interrupted by Kawai's father, Thomas stumbled over his words and feet en route to the car. As the two started their journey to forever, Thomas's passenger side tire had other plans. A quick change to the spare, and they were off again, this time being stopped by the local police, with a frustrated Thomas extending the interaction. After Kawai talked them out of a ticket and Thomas a night in the hoosegow, he realized there was a better chance of Hitler pulling troops out of Britain than making their reservations.

Kawai was clueless about why Thomas was so upset since their evening had just started. Sure, a flat tire and interaction with O'ahu's finest wasn't exactly her idea of fun, but the night was far from over, and like she always did, Kawai was determined to flip the mood back into a hopeful one.

"What's wrong?" Kawai asked as she reached for Thomas's hand with a smile. "Those cops would never give you a hard time with me in the car; besides, we have our entire night still to enjoy."

"I just wanted tonight to be perfect for you," Thomas said as he turned towards Kawai as the two waited for the red light to flip back to green. "I made reservations at the winery, hoping to spark that passion you had talking about the future last night. I've never heard someone be so hopeful about what possibilities could be waiting for them, and I just wanted to hear more."

"Thomas Metic, get rid of that frown," Kawai demanded as she set up on her knees, facing him. "If you are going to be part of my future, you will have to take any negative situation with a grain of salt and do whatever you can to turn that into sweet, sweet sugar. I'm flattered that you did all of that for me, but even if we just sat in this hot car and talked all night, it would be as special as any fancy dinner. Now, let's get some stuff for a picnic and head to the beach that seemed as magical as we could ask last night. Why change it?"

"You're right," Thomas said with a grin. "I just know when I'm in the sky, I'm in control of a lot of what happens to me, especially during training. It's different with you."

"Not every situation with us will be positive," Kawai said as she ran her fingers through his. "But, if we do everything in our control to remain upbeat, we will realize that every day was a good one when we lay our heads down at night. Tonight will be unforgettable, and tomorrow, you will pick me up at 7:00, take me to the winery, buy me a glass of wine, and it will be as if none of the negative events from tonight never happened."

"That sounds perfect."

After a quick trip to his barracks to grab a few cheap bottles of wine from Lance's stash, and while Kawai ran into the market for their picnic cuisine, they quickly fell into each other's arms as the sun set on another flawless Hawaiian evening.

CHAPTER 3

Thomas and Kawai had no idea of the horror that laid in the weeds twelve hours from the moment they returned to the beach. Even with that impending reality, neither of them could fathom anything but falling just a little bit more in love with each passing second.

The waves splashed with the sun resting to the west as Thomas struggled to open the bottle he stole from Lance's closest. Kawai laid in the sand, watching him, with a smile that hadn't left her face since Thomas first spoke to her. He was the first American guy she ever met that wasn't cocky and over-confident. Thomas gave the impression that he was lucky to be in her presence and had so much pressure on himself to leave an excellent first impression. Even though he failed in that endeavor, he left an even deeper stamp on her heart.

"Why did you struggle so bad talking to me yesterday?" Kawai asked as Thomas finally was able to pour her a drink.

"We talked all night," Thomas said with a confused look.

"No, silly, the first time," Kawai said with a laugh as she took a sip. "You were like a toddler trying to ask for candy 'uh, um, can I, uh.' Why was that?"

"What do you mean why," Thomas began with a surprised glare. "I know you don't have a ton of free time, but I'm sure you look in the mirror a few times a day. Next time you do, ask yourself why I may have struggled to talk to you."

"That's not why," Kawai said as she moved closer, moving Thomas's arms so she could sit between them. "I've seen hundreds of nurses, read thousands of magazines with American women from cover to cover. America is known to have the world's most beautiful women; you've grown up around all of that and see nurses all day long."

"For one, apparently Hawaii has the most beautiful women in the world," Thomas said as he held her. "For two, you're unlike anyone I've ever seen in my life. No woman has the smile you do, which glows brighter than a new Cadillac. Their hair doesn't lay as effortlessly as yours does. It didn't matter how busy of a day at work you had yesterday; as soon as you let your hair down, it was naturally perfect- straight, or curly, it doesn't matter. We're training for war, a worldwide conflict, and none of those nurses could give less of a damn. In a few short months, all their lives could be on the line, and they wouldn't be as well trained as they could have been. They don't care to put in the work. But you? You put in the work every single day to survive for yourself and your family. You put every spec of blood, drop of sweat, and wiped away tear into that theater, no matter how unappreciative those nurses that you think so highly of are. You're the hardest working person on this island, and the first day I walked into that theater, I knew that right away."

"Even with everything you said, I'm just a regular person," Kawai said as she ran her fingers through Thomas's. "Is there something about me that made you that nervous to talk to me? Your friend seems to have no problem talking to any woman he passes; believe me, I've seen him in action."

"Lance? He doesn't care what kind of impression he leaves," Thomas said, passion building in his voice. "He grew up with a family that didn't even realize the Great Depression was a thing. Lance joined up to show his father and mother he could make his way, but really, it's just his means to a good party. He's not searching for anything in a woman, just a good time."

"Were you searching for something when you met me?" Kawai asked as she looked into his eyes.

"I didn't realize it at the moment, but I guess I have been for some time," Thomas said while scratching his head. "When I was a kid, my grandma helped my grandad on the farm. She did everything- feed the cattle, plant the fields, chores... *everything,* which wasn't common around other families. When the families from the town would get together or cross paths, all the men would give my grandma the most defeating looks, acting as if her efforts meant nothing and she was just a pretty face behind a man that was doing the work. That couldn't have been further from the truth. She was the reason for every bit of success our family had, but instead of arguing or stating her case, as I often wished she did, she would just smile, sometimes shake their hands, and get back to work. The first time I went to the theater, Lance dragged me out. It was my first time going out since I was stationed at Pearl, and he already had a date waiting for me. When I opened those doors and saw you doing three tasks simultaneously while everyone in line was rude and impatient, you kept the biggest, most beautiful smile on your face. It took me back to seeing my grandma wear the same smile. The same strength."

"I don't know what to say," Kawai uttered.

"That was the first moment I believed in the possibility of being with someone," Thomas said after a few moments of silence. "You made me feel like I did when my grandparents would tell stories of their early years together without even meeting you. Your life had a purpose, and you had passion. Anyone looking at the situation from afar could see the fear of the unknown in your eyes. Yet, all you did was provide a few seconds of positivity and hope to everyone you talked to. Seeing that changed my perspective, whether I ended up talking to you or not, that's probably why I struggled so much to speak to you yesterday. I struggled because talking to you meant something to me, something I didn't fully understand, but that I knew made me feel complete for the first time since I was a little boy."

"I'm glad you told me that," Kawai said as she sat up, facing Thomas. "I guess we don't know the effect we have or can have on people we've only met in passing. Times are tough at the theater, and I deal with my fair share of rude customers, whether they're people I've known my whole life or Americans. When that all overwhelms me, I find a few minutes to sit away from the pressure, close my eyes and think of nights in the garden when my mom would lay my head on her lap, play with my hair, and tell me I could be whatever I wanted to be when I grew up. That made me feel empowered. But when I grew older, I realized that while those evenings with my mother were happening, she and my father were holding onto our business, home, *everything* by a string. Until I was a teen, I had no idea we were ever struggling, and that was because my mom did everything with a smile and a sense of hope. She made me believe I could do anything I wanted, and no matter what cards, people, or circumstances are stacked up against me, I find my happiness in thoughts of her smile and wisdom. When you see me facing challenges with a grin, that's her strength coming out of me."

"Like mother, like daughter," Thomas said, "I have a feeling I'm going to be thinking of your smile, positive attitude, and passion when times get tough in my life from now on, too. I'll have to thank Mrs. Mehelona for raising the perfect woman."

"You're not so bad yourself, Mr. Metic," Kawai said with a half-smile. "I grew up in a family where I was to be seen, not heard other than those nights spent with my mother. I'm sure that is pretty normal, but in my family and as I grew older, it has seemed to be just a theme in my life. As soon as I could understand how to do the job, my dad had me sweeping floors, then bagging popcorn and checking people out for tickets. My life has been one day after another of head down, no talking, very little dreaming, just trying to make it to the next bill cycle above water. Sure, I still have dreams and aspirations, but until last night, since my mom when I was young, no one had ever taken the time to sit with me and care about what I had to say about anything. In school, I was just the poor girl who had to work and could never go out. Boys didn't like that; they wanted a girl to go surfing with or explore the mountains with, and it became easy for my friends to forget about me since I was never around outside of school. In my life, I just became the girl who worked and kept to herself. You made me feel like I was the most interesting person you had ever talked to last night, like I mattered and could do anything I wanted to. You made my heart race when I thought about running the winery, and honestly, you made me think about the possibility of love, which I hadn't had time to even think about since I was a young girl. You listen to me, Thomas, and hear me when I speak. You make me feel alive, like my life has a purpose outside of the four walls of the theater, like I am the main character to a featured film, not a ticket saleswoman in O'ahu."

The sun was nearly unrecognizable, with a slight mist in the air from the waves crashing beneath their feet, as Kawai and Thomas's lips met for the first time. The water grew fuller around their bodies as the tide began rolling in. Minutes and dry clothes passed, as the two of them lost themselves in each other's touch.

Peace fell over them both, with the tension of the moment gone. As they laid in the wet O'ahu sand, with the moonlight making them the center of a Hollywood love story, their heartbeats joined in perfect harmony, matching the native crickets and katydids in the distance. Thomas could feel Kawai's racing heartbeat as he placed his hand on her cheek and through her hair. It seemed as if all their struggles in life were pushing them towards this moment. Every friend lost because of a double-shift or Christmas morning ruined by unfaithful and drunk parents had built a passion in Thomas and Kawai's souls that came out in a magical evening.

"How will you protect me if a baby crab scares you?" Kawai said with an uncontrollable laugh as a small crab raced across Thomas's foot, causing him to jump.

"It was this big!" she said, demonstrating how significant the crab was.

"We don't have anything like those in Pennsylvania, and the Navy sure as hell didn't train me for that," Thomas responded, out of breath.

"You're lucky you're handsome," Kawai said with a snort.

"Was that what I think it was?" Thomas asked as he moved close to her.

"Don't worry about it," Kawai shouted as she playfully ran towards the water, away from Thomas.

Most look across the ocean to the looming horizon, lit by moonlight, with a sense of peace. There could be anything where the sky and water meet, any possibility you could dream up, confidence and determination for what came next. Thomas had only felt that peace when daydreaming about his job as a pilot- since being stationed at Pearl, looking at every passing mile from his cockpit. As he chased Kawai into the water, starring into her big brown eyes, *that* is where he found real hope and possibility. Unlike the feeling most got in their belly looking over the water, the sense Thomas found in Kawai's maple eyes was strong enough to last a lifetime.

It was a prominent building of love, and a speechless feeling neither had ever experienced in their young lives. They didn't know what was next. Another rent payment missed, or maybe a new training session to overcome slow, hand-me-down planes when the war for America finally kicked off, could be their reality when the sun rose. No matter what tomorrow held or what losing hand they were dealt next, the two would take it on together. No longer were they the hard-working, quiet Hawaiian girl or the strait-laced Naval pilot. They were a team. Nothing else mattered.

"It's only been two days, Thomas, but I want every night to end just like this," Kawai said while she rang out her soaked hair as the two of them sat on a peer.

"Ended like what?" Thomas said with a sarcastic grin. "You ringing out your hair and me drying my boots?"

"Maybe so. Is that not okay?" Kawai said, matching Thomas's sarcasm. "No, I mean with you, enjoying every sunset together until our eyes grow so old, we can't see it anymore. I'm worried, however, that tomorrow, or even the one we just watched, could be our last sunset together for a while. That everything we have built in just a few nights could be put on pause."

"Why are you talking like that?" Thomas asked as he held her hand between both of his.

"I read the newspaper, Thomas," Kawai said as she looked through him. "I know things in Europe are getting worse, and Hitler will never be peaceful. We may not go to war with the Nazis directly, but I know you're up there preparing like we are every day. You could be transferred tomorrow at the drop of a hat, and I'm a local girl... a nobody... not a nurse, so you wouldn't even be guaranteed to say goodbye to me."

"Kawai, the fact that we're together on this beach right now, is a miracle," Thomas said as he reached to brush a stray hair on her face away. "We come from two extremely different places, with contrasting backgrounds and personalities, yet here we are. Whenever I feel your touch, smell your perfume or stare into your eyes, my heart jumps out of my chest. It doesn't matter if the military sent me to the moon; I would never leave you behind. Every waking minute away for you would be spent planning and crossing off the moments until I could hold you again. The feeling I have inside of me, that shield around my heart that is your touch, something I've been searching for, for as long as I can remember, even if I hadn't realized that until now. I don't care what it takes, what adversity I have to go through, that *we* have to go through, it doesn't matter, you are mine, and I am yours, forever and always. I've never been so sure of anything in my life."

"I bet you have more confidence in Lance showing up to training on Monday hungover," Kawai said with an emotional chuckle as tears filled her eyes. "I trust you, and for some reason, I trust this."

Doubt was, of course, in Kawai's mind, *both of their minds*; it had only been two days since Thomas thought he had ruined the whole thing during their first conversation. Not even two complete trips around the sun, and they were both deeply in love- a short romance, quicker than any barrel roll or rush into the theater for seats. The chances of them making it were slim, but the chances of them meeting in the first place were even slimmer, and they had already beaten those odds with flying colors. There was a war on, a struggling economy, and relations between their people at odds, but the unlikely love, was pure, and with possible death or poverty at every turn, that's all either of them could ask for.

"Since you want to be with me forever," Kawai said, moving her head side-to-side as she looked into Thomas's light green eyes. "You should know that I was a twin. My brother was born just a few minutes before me. Kahuna was his name."

"Was?" Thomas asked with uncertainty.

"He passed away when we were a few days old, and I grew up an only child," Kawai said as she turned her head towards the black, dimly moonlit sea. "Kahuna means 'a secret,' which is precisely what I've kept of his memory and how my family has viewed his life. I've never spoken about him, not to my mother, father, friends, no one. I promised myself that the first person I told would be the first man that gained my trust enough to know, which is you."

"You're as brave as anyone," Thomas said, unsure of what was the right thing to say. "That must be hard to carry around with you and not share with anyone. You shouldn't have to hold on to that and live in that pain alone. I'm here, and I know it may be premature to say this, but I'm proud of you."

"Thank you, but that's not why I told you," she said with a nervous smile. "I want kids, and if I can't have twins, I want two children close in age to grow up together. They will have each other's back no matter what. Experience vacations, pets, heartbreak, discipline, lessons, and everything else we will throw their way, side-by-side. If I can have this, watch them grow up, anything else will be a plus."

"My dream doesn't exist without grandkids, so kids it is," Thomas said as he leaned to kiss Kawai on the cheek, hoping to ease her anxious feelings. "Twins run in my family, too. My grandma and her father were twins; maybe it will skip a few generations, and we will get lucky. Anything is possible if you believe."

"I believe I'll beat you to the water," Kawai laughed as she pushed Thomas away and took off running, with her dress blowing in the wind.

The night was filled with meaningful, anxiously driven conversations, with each passing hour feeling quicker than the previous. They both feared what the future might hold, even if they didn't always verbalize those fears. Would Kawai's family accept Thomas as the man for their daughter if things got more serious than a few nights on the beach? Could the United States dive head-first into an unwinnable war in Europe? Thomas wouldn't get transferred just months after arriving at Pearl, right? The economy is getting better, isn't it? Factors, some in their control, most not, were pushing toward Kawai and Thomas with such force, but the love they were building was enough, even if just for the night, to keep all of that at bay.

Thomas stopped in his tracks as he approached Kawai, a few steps into the water, as she began to undo her dress and throw it to the side. Every moment of Thomas's childhood and time in the Navy had prepared him to deal with anything he came across in life, but there was no planning for this. The woman he would take a bullet for, run a marathon to kiss, and protect from an entire army with everything he had, stood in front of him, wearing only undergarments and an excitable smile. Her energy gave Thomas the confidence to stand with her, chest to chest, tremble for tremble.

"Are you sure—" Thomas asked as Kawai interrupted him, placing her finger over his shaking lips.

"Shh, yes," Kawai replied anxiously as she leaned in for a soft kiss, hoping Thomas was as sure as she was.

Weak knees gave out to wet sand as their now bare bodies met with just a glimpse of the Hawaii sunrise creeping in from the East. Mentally, their love for each other had been played out for hours. Physically, their love was finally being made under a star-filled sky. Nothing was between their bodies now, as their inexperience was on full display. There was no book on how to turn your love for the woman of your dreams from emotional to physical; everything was from the soul. Every kiss was gentle, touch playful, and unimaginable, like a stroke on a canvas to the most beautiful landscape.

Though it was over as quickly as it began, their love was justified in both of their minds. It was fast, everything about their passion seemed accelerated, but that was just a byproduct of their surroundings. They both had an idea that the most challenging days of their lives were in front of them, not behind, which was terrifying, given the struggles they had both overcome. Sex wasn't only an activity for them, like it was for Lance or other pilots, living every second like his last. It was another step on their journey to forever. Some spend weeks connecting with their person, some months, other's years. For Kawai and Thomas, it was only a few days.

Their bodies laid interlocked with only a thin blanket around them. Kawai's head on Thomas's chest, with her leg wrapped around his lower body, as they turned themselves towards the dark orange sky appearing in the east. The dawn of another day was upon their fairytale, and neither had any obligations or agenda. Therefore, all they had was time and no reason to waste any of it on sleep.

Kawai wasn't one for patience, only admiring the music of Thomas's breathing and heartbeat for a few minutes before wrapping herself in a blanket, putting her dress back on, and jumping onto her knees to face Thomas's fatigued body.

"Wake up," she said with her famous smile. "Let's talk about baby names; I know it is years away, but I've been thinking about that moment since I can remember. So, can we?"

"I am awake," Thomas said with a smirk. "Anything for you. Any ideas?"

"I'd like to name our boy after Kahuna," Kawai said, hoping Thomas would approve. "For our girl, what about a name from your family, maybe after your grandma?"

"You're confident in us having a boy and a girl, aren't you?" Thomas asked as he set up and sat in front of Kawai, stealing a kiss on his way up.

"We will have to keep trying until we do," Kawai demanded. "So, what do you think?"

"I love trying with you, so yes," Thomas said with a laugh. "As for the names, I love them too, and I'd love even more if our future son or sons carried on your brother's memory. My grandma's name was Elizabeth, and so is my mother's middle name, so I'd be fine with Beth for short, to honor my grandmother, but not glorify my mom; plus, it will be unique, you don't hear the name 'Beth,' much."

The rest of their life together was planned, down to the kids that would carry their last name and hear stories of the love developed beneath the stars and wrapped in the sand. The sun was almost completely visible as Kawai and Thomas walked towards a nearby boardwalk, which led to a few diners and shops near the base, hoping they could grab a nice breakfast before the Sunday morning rush commenced. As they approached a small diner, getting prepped for opening, Kawai stopped Thomas, reaching to undo the necklace that rested against her chest. It was a Floating Brown Pearl Necklace that had been passed down from Kawai's great-grandmother to her grandma, mother, and then to her when she was a little girl. The pearl was alone at the bale, accompanied by a string around the neck, with tiny wood beads resting above the base, each with carved initials of the women who came before Kawai, hers, and a blank place for her first-born daughter.

"Take this," Kawai said to Thomas as she balled it neatly together, placing it in his hand. "I don't know what tomorrow holds, and no matter how confident you are in us always being together, neither do you. I want to be with you wherever you go. If you get transferred, travel one day for a job, or go stateside without me to visit family, I'll always be with you, and God forbid they take you away from me and throw you into a war that doesn't even concern us, this will keep you safe. It has survived the hardships of my people, a financial collapse, and many personal struggles. My great-grandma and grandma died older women, and my mother is in better health than most. It will be our strength, no matter what we face, but you need it with you right now."

"I don't know what to say," Thomas uttered as he moved toward Kawai to embrace her.

The ground beneath them began to shake, interrupting their moment, with screams in the distance becoming louder with each passing second. As they turned towards the commotion, they could see a sea of massive red dots painted on the sides of a fleet of low, passing planes. Green, white, and silver planes zoomed past at speeds almost too fast to recognize. In the distance, Lance came towards Kawai and Thomas, shirt unbuttoned, bare chest already covered in sweat, sprinting at a clip that seemed almost faster than the planes soaring above him. What was happening was too surreal to understand. As Lance approached them, Thomas and Kawai were frozen in place; heads turned upward.

"Thomas, let's go," Lance shouted as he pulled Thomas away. "The Japanese are here, and they aren't leaving anytime soon. We need to report to General Quarter asap!"

Thomas said nothing, pushing Lance away, as he stared through Kawai, who was also being ushered. A clerk at the diner was pulling Kawai inside the restaurant as she fought to free herself, with tears of fear and confusion running down both cheeks. Explosions began in the distance, one torpedo after another, and though he had a job to accomplish, all Thomas wanted to do was pick Kawai up and run to somewhere safe. Somewhere they could talk about how big the porch around their future home would be, what their children's personalities may be like, and where they would take them on their first family vacation. Taking his place in a war that had only played on the big screen wasn't where Thomas imagined himself just moments before.

"I'll meet you back here at 7:00 tonight, no later," Thomas shouted from Lance's pulling arms as he began to turn away from Kawai. "I'll never leave you; I promise. Forever and always, remember that."

"I love you," Kawai said softly through her quavering lips, knowing Thomas would never be able to hear her, as she fell to her knees in the diner doorway.

CHAPTER 4

Black smoke replaced bright blue skies. Sounds of waves crashing and trees blowing in the wind were muffled by bombs piercing destroyers and screams of the men trapped inside. Street cars and Hawaiian shirts were replaced by military transport and officer uniforms. America's worst nightmare was a shocking reality to most. Peace with Japan had been a naive expectation, and now, they had to survive a battle no one was prepared for.

Panic ravaged everyone's minds. Hope wasn't easily found for those manning battle stations on Battleship Row, to pilots strapping into planes that never left the ground and nurses maneuvering bullets falling from the sky like pouring rain. For Thomas, the past 48-hours had given him enough hope for a lifetime, and there was a clear goal in his mind as he ran: find his way back to Kawai.

Thomas and Lance bolted from the boardwalk through swampy hills and dry fields, picking their way from cover to cover. Their hearts beat out of their chests, but not the way Thomas had experienced just hours before as he made love to the woman of his dreams. This time, it was because of the fear that he may never see her again. Though preparation taught Thomas and Lance to make their way to an airfield, find a few unharmed planes, fire them up and provide some air support to fight the Japanese. The reality was that they were just trying to survive.

Every soldier, sailor or pilot has a call to action when all hell breaks loose: a duty to serve, help who they can, and defend what is theirs. On December 7th, 1941, Thomas Metic and Lance Jones were late in their efforts to assist.

The two made their way back to base in just under an hour. In showing up largely undetected by hundreds of Japanese aircraft, they realized every plane they had trained in and tweaked for better performance was destroyed. Many men they had trained with and looked forward to serving alongside had perished trying to organize a defense against goliath. Everyone lucky enough to survive had either fled for cover or went elsewhere to help.

With no transportation or ammunition to defend themselves, there was no way to get to Battleship Row or lay down cover fire for any potential air support. Neither Thomas nor Lance had ever felt a helplessness like the one resting inside them. They signed up to defend the country against all threats, foreign and domestic, but all they could do was watch from afar.

What was left of a dreadful hour stay in hell passed; Thomas and Lance had finally made their way to a local clinic. As they went inside, it was overrun with wounded soldiers. Chaplin's giving last rights. Nurses picking who to make comfortable and who to try to save. Men were crying out for their mothers one minute, then asking what had happened the next. The room was full of blood, helplessness, and confusion.

A nurse calmly led them to a nearby station, where they spent as much time as they could holding the hands of their fellow airmen and sailors while giving much-needed blood. As Thomas sat there, I.V. in his left arm, right hand around a dying soldier's fingers, regret filled his mind. Regretful, he left home and gave up on his mother. Repentant, he never thanked his grandparents for all they had done for him, and most of all, disappointed, he left Kawai's arms as quickly as he entered them.

Thomas felt embarrassed that the only contribution he had made all day was giving a few pints of blood and being the last voice a fellow soldier heard before being called home. Though those were honorable and essential tasks, he didn't turn the engine over on his plane, pull a trigger, or lead even one man into battle. The love of his life had been ripped from his arms without warning and a moment he'd trained for his whole life was over before he could leave his mark.

Before Thomas could sink deeper into his thoughts, Lance and himself were in the back of a car, finally on their way to Battleship Row, hoping to help the men trapped inside destroyers and locate those missing in action. Each minute that passed and mile that went by, their nightmares cemented into reality. Every step taken from the car to the USS Arizona, desperate cries for help from men inside grew louder.

Neither Thomas, Lance, nor the hundreds of other sailors and airman attempting to help could do anything for the men trapped inside. Tallies of MIA to KIA seemed to double and triple by the hour, and as the afternoon passed, thousands were confirmed dead. Early evening was spent cleaning up, hugging those lucky enough to survive, and toasting those not so fortunate. Aided by a lack of sleep and seeing things he wouldn't wish on anyone, Thomas began to ponder his worth.

"I'd rather be dead than do nothing at all," Thomas thought to himself, sitting at a bar alone, wondering whether to order a drink. *"I should have been there. I should have been awoken by the first wave like my brothers were. I should have fought right beside them until my last breath, not held their hands while they took theirs, and I carried on."*

"What are you doing," Lance shouted as he ran up to Thomas. "I've been looking for you. Aren't you supposed to meet Kawai at seven by the diner?"

"Shit, Kawai," Thomas whispered as he stumbled off the barstool and out the door.

Thomas sprinted toward the diner, fighting off sickness from the fatigue, lack of food, and horror that the sunset he was staring at would be his first away from Kawai. How could he forget about her? How could the one he started the day poised to return to be the first thing that slipped his mind when things got tough? The woman he made love to, hoped to marry, and couldn't wait to hold her hand as she gave birth to their children one day, became a footnote in his mind.

Through everything he had seen and experienced over the last twelve hours of his life, nothing compared to the sadness and panic Thomas felt as he ran. No breaks or pauses for a breath. Miles went by, and Thomas approached the diner, praying to whoever would listen that Kawai would be there to greet him. He spoke endlessly to his lord and savior, begged his grandparents for a miracle, and apologized for everything he had done wrong. Thomas vowed never to leave Kawai again, forget about her even for a second or go another minute without telling her exactly how he felt.

Thomas approached the diner with half of the building missing, windows blown out, and shingles lacing the floor. As Thomas searched through the diner and nearby businesses, Kawai was nowhere to be found. He ran up-and-down the beach looking for her and asking where she was. Military personnel were too overwhelmed to care, and locals were too scared to give over any information. What was left of the sunlight had passed, and Thomas fell to his knees against the tide, washing what was left of a days' worth of disappointment off his body, sobbing at thoughts of what might be.

His guilt-filled, blood and sweat-coated body fell flat in the sand as he reached into his pocket for the Brown pearl necklace Kawai had given him earlier that day. It seemed like a lifetime ago that she handed the necklace to him and told him it would keep him safe. She was correct; he made it through the day. But did she?

Thomas drifted in and out of sleep, with nightmare after nightmare about what he had seen, where Kawai was, and visions of how she might have gone. One minute he hoped she had died suddenly, with minimal suffering. The next, he clenched the necklace, convincing himself that she just didn't make it back to their safe spot and he would be reunited with her when the sun came up.

Where was she? Who was she with? Was she scared, sad, or alone? Maybe someone had gone after her to tell her Thomas was safe. Could she be searching for him, just like he had been trying to find her? Thomas raced to his feet, moving a few steps before his energy-less body hit the sand, once again, like a punch from a professional boxer. As he fought his way onto his back, Thomas did everything to focus his eyes on the stars above, holding tight to Kawai's initials on the necklace rim. The fatigue was too bearing, and he drifted into a fast sleep, dreaming of evenings from another life.

"When you find someone like your grandma, you hold onto her," Thomas's grandpa's voice echoed through his mind. "No matter what, you protect her, respect her, and never forget her. No accomplishment in this world compares to each time you hold her hand. Each day, hour, and minute wrapped in her arms is a blessing. When you find that, you hold on to that and never give up on her."

"Thomas, Thomas, let's go," Lance shouted as he shook Thomas's water-stained body awake. "We have to report at 0730. Get up!"

Before they knew it, Lance and Thomas, ruined clothes, shaggy hair, and all, were in a room full of other sailors and airmen, pondering what was next. It didn't matter that all Thomas wanted to do was cover every inch of the island looking for Kawai. He hadn't even been given a chance to visit her home yet; he and everyone else once again had a job to do.

A hanger had been cleared of some of the only useable equipment left from the day before, chairs lined in a corner in the front, with an empty chalk board at the center. Lance and Thomas were the last of their squadron to arrive, which had been cut thin from those who perished. Usually, everyone would be laughing and joking with Thomas about his outfit, making assumptions about what the night before had been like for him and why he might look the way he did. No one dared to speak a word now. The truth was, nobody looked their best or had slept more than a few hours. They all were in the same boat: confused, scared, determined, and anxious about what they were about to hear.

"Alright, fellas," Commander Styles said as he rushed in front of his men. "Pretty simple; we're all confused, pissed off, and maybe a little scared of what's next. We all signed up to protect this land, that flag, and the ideals we all left back home. That duty begins today. As you'd expect, our morning and afternoon will be spent at funerals and memorials for those lost. After that, we will give blood and assist at the hospital, meet back here for a dinner, drink, and briefing, and then we're out of here on a plane, covered by darkness. You'll learn where we're going when we get there. Save your questions for then. Today, we will spend together. Plan some time to write home tonight before we leave; there's no telling when you will get another letter out."

Just like that, Thomas knew the last time he would see Kawai, for at least a few months, would be in front of the diner, terrified of what was happening and doing everything she could to run into his arms. All he wanted was to hold her, kiss her and reassure her that they would never leave each other's side again. Thomas couldn't help but think if he and Kawai's love story was over before it really began with every memorial he visited, casket he walked by, and story he heard.

Thomas's heart broke for those lost, their friends left behind to fight on, but at least they all had closure. Those people had the closure of knowing what had happened to the person they cared about. For all Thomas knew, Kawai was out looking for him, and in just a few hours, he'd be on a plane to a top-secret location.

Thoughts of going AWOL, fleeing the squadron, and searching for the only family he had, raced across Thomas's mind. What's the worst that could happen if he fled? Imprisonment? It didn't matter. Nothing compared to the sense of emptiness that consumed every inch of his body.

One minute, Thomas felt guilty. Even though it was out of his control, if he stayed with the squadron, he would be placed on a plane to only God knows where, doing what only the United States Navy wanted. He was leaving, leaving the woman of his dreams behind to fight her own battle... or her family to deal with the death of their daughter. Not knowing if she was dead or alive, missing or found, made the idea of leaving or staying with his brothers even harder.

On the other hand, like Commander Styles said, they all signed up to protect and defend the people of the United States of America. Nobody knew what was next. No one knew where they would be shipped out to at night's end, but what they did know was the job they had to do, and Thomas was no different. He spent most of his childhood, especially his teen years, dreaming of serving in the World's Greatest Navy, climbing the ladder, and leading a group of men. The opportunity to do that had never been more significant, and though Thomas led himself to believe he had a decision to make, between Kawai or the Navy. He didn't.

"Thomas, come here and let me talk to you a second," Lance said as he prepared for a rare moment of seriousness. "Look, I know I don't take these things nearly as serious as I should, or you'd like me to, but listen to me for a minute, brother to brother. When I woke up yesterday and ran up to you, I thought I'd recognize the guy I was searching for. The guy I've trained beside, the Thomas I know. Since he landed at Pearl, he's been plotting his strategy and leadership, daydreaming about owning dog fight after dog fight in the sky. The guy I ended up coming across yesterday and the one standing across me today... isn't him."

"It's not that simple. You don't have it all figured out," Thomas argued as he pointed at Lance sternly.

"Listen," Lance said, walking even closer to Thomas. "I know you love her; I see it in your eyes right now, but we have a job to do. I wish I could stay here with you and travel up and down this island until we find her, but neither of us can do that. We don't have a choice; you don't have a choice, Thomas. It's time to serve and do what we signed up to do. That's not what you want to hear, and I know that, but I believe that you will see her again one day. She's alive, and I believe that, but right now, we have to fight, and I need my wingman."

Thomas couldn't hold in what he was feeling anymore; keep a straight face and carry on. He pulled Lance tight, sobbing into his shoulder. The days his grandparents were called home hurt. When he found out his mom was unfaithful and his dad was drinking his life away cut like a knife, but the pain and uncertainty he felt in this moment was unlike anything before. There were days during the Great Depression when the Metic household didn't know where their next meal would come from, but the aches in Thomas's stomach as he embraced Lance were the worst pain he'd ever felt.

Kawai was in every scenario he pictured for his future. Whether in Hawaii, Pennsylvania, or somewhere in between, he'd be by her side, on a wrap-around porch, with their beautiful kids playing in the yard. Life would be perfect because they would be together, no matter where they were. When Thomas assured Kawai, lying beside her on the beach, that they would never leave each other's side, he knew better, and so did she. Active duty, training, something would eventually split them up. Neither would say it, but they both understood it. All Thomas wished as he packed his bags for a trip to hell was that he would have a chance to see Kawai again.

CHAPTER 5

"Metic, you're up, let's go," a man said forcefully as Thomas took his seat.

It was December 9th, just past midnight and exactly 41-hours since Thomas had left Kawai at the diner steps. Thomas had barely seen the back of his eyelids in days, and even though the sky was dark, he could still see a glaze in the clouds left behind by the Japanese. Sounds of men yelling desperately from the Arizona played on rewind in his exhausted mind. Tired was an understatement, but sleeping was an afterthought.

Hundreds of men lined the rows, but Thomas felt alone. It was as if the plane was empty, and the thin belt across his lap was a ball-and-chain, forcing him into a battle he didn't want to be a part of. The months before meeting Kawai, all Thomas cared about was preparing for a war he hoped never came. During those two magical nights on the O'ahu beach, he didn't think once of the possibility of war or how he'd survive it.

Commander Styles did his best to convince the men to prepare themselves for what they may experience next, but that was the furthest thing from Thomas's mind. Maybe some could do that, but Thomas was still in Hawaii, and no matter how many miles the plane traveled, or how many minutes ticked by like sand in an hourglass, his mind was with Kawai. She was all he cared about, and no matter how bad it made Thomas feel that he wasn't focused on the war, he couldn't lie to himself.

Thomas knew his feelings for Kawai were real as he sat, staring into the seat in front of him, hand placed gently against the belt, because there was nothing around him to remind him of her. There was no sunset to remind him of their first kiss, popcorn stand to make him laugh, and especially no moonlight, through the dark clouds. Nothing outside his window seat reminded him of Kawai, yet his mind fabricated those painful memories of love possibly lost.

He tried to convince himself that she wouldn't be just a memory. The last time they laid eyes on each other, panicked and terrified, wouldn't be the final time they spoke, but those were wishful thoughts. Thomas, nor anyone around him, knew of any local's condition, and outside of Lance, none of them knew of his relationship with Kawai.

Their love was a shotgun romance, unexpected and even more so, undetected. Those around Thomas never viewed him as the romantic type- the soldier to leave his duties behind for a night out and a good story in the morning light. That wasn't him. Thomas was the first one in, the last one out, and present every moment in-between. No one would have considered Thomas having a love interest, and if they did, everyone would expect him to put that second to the battle in front of them.

Thomas spent most of his life waiting for the day he could sign the dotted line and join the United States Navy. Everything he did after his grandparents passed away led him to that moment. Every fight his parents had, every night without a meal, bill missed, pushed him further away from them and closer to the battle. He never let himself think of the pain he was going through internally, the struggle that he had been battling in his mind since his grandma and grandpa were called home wasn't even on his radar.

Each time an adverse event happened, Thomas would shove it deep down, go to sleep and wake up to check another day between him and the wide-open horizons off. The Navy wasn't just a safe place to lay his head at night and three hot meals. It wasn't only a tight schedule and clear goal in mind, or wide-open spaces in the sky. It was structure he had been yearning for since his early teens.

The Navy and training for war was the lantern that held a trauma-filled candle. A candle that burned for years without stopping was suddenly washed to darkness by the bluest of oceans, fastest planes, and bravest men. Training for battle was all Thomas knew and all he had longed for since leaving Pennsylvania. Everything that had happened in his childhood had been pushed as deep as he could get it and not brought up. The other men were just like him, too busy to care about the past. There was a job to do and a country they were assigned to defend.

When Thomas stumbled through talking to Kawai for the first time, his path was forever altered. No longer were his feelings buried. For the first time in years, he thought about and expressed his feelings for his grandparents. Thomas spoke about his mother's sleepless nights in other men's beds and his dad's drunken evenings on the broken-down porch, sipping the family's savings away.

Before Kawai, everyone Thomas cared to protect was right beside him. In his mind, the family he still had wouldn't care if he lived or died, so their well-being was an afterthought. Thomas was at ease if the man on his left, and the one on his right returned home when the training session or battle was over. After Kawai, like the sun, Thomas's life revolved around her.

Regret played in the circumstances. Time was moving slower than a plane down a cylinder, but during the few days before the attack, it flew faster than life changes. In the blink of an eye, Thomas went from focusing on himself and his squadron, to planning his life with the woman of a dream he didn't know existed. She was everything, and it took meeting her, then losing her, to realize that. Like most, Thomas didn't understand what he had until it was gone.

Should he have wrestled out of Lance's arms and stayed with her? Gone through everything she did, ran with her, cried with her, died or survived with her. Was he selfish for doing his job? Would she forgive him or wait for him to return if she was still alive?

Unrealistic scenarios repeatedly played in Thomas's tired mind, but he realized that Kawai made the Navy and the men alongside him mean less. Family was everything again. She returned him to the hopeful little boy, in overalls and a dirty hat, enjoying an ice cream cone on his grandpa's lap. Every minute with her was a possibility for something astonishing. Each time their eyes met, lips touched, and bodies brushed, the unknown of tomorrow became exciting. From head down, fighting for his men, to head up, looking in the eyes of the only family he had left, someone new to love emerged, and rebirth was possible.

He was a better pilot now, and as unsure as everything around him had become, that was clear. Thomas had something bigger than himself and his men to worry about. Commander Styles preached day in and day out about what helped him through the Western Front of The Great War. It was family. His wife, kids, hell, even pets pushed him to be better, care more, and worry less. They were in his heart, protected by God, and all they wanted was for him to return home. For years, each man Thomas trained to protect had something he didn't. On the eve of that training being tested, he too found it; it was love.

In attempting to piece all of his loose feelings together with hours of his trip to World War II passing, Thomas searched for wisdom in his grandpa's memory. Evenings on his lap as a kid taught Thomas more about love than any relationship. Lessons were learned from afar, as Thomas's grandpa painted a picture of 1800s, post-Civil War Pennsylvania. Days in the mill led to late nights sitting across from the most beautiful waitress at a small, rundown diner on the edge of town. First conversations, dates, and a love built to withstand hardship came and lasted forever. A family and mutual dreams were formed. Long hours built the foundation of a farm passed down to Thomas's mother. They created a life together from nothing. Thomas could only hope for his chance to do the same with Kawai.

A chance to fight for every penny, save enough to buy the winery Kawai dreamed about and a small farm that appeared in Thomas's daydreams. Hard work, dedication, and an unbreakable love built everything his grandparents had, and Thomas knew if Kawai and himself were given a fair chance, they could have the same.

With nearly all his peers around him asleep, and very little light to be seen, Thomas closed his eyes but not to sleep. He imagined those evenings, with the sun stretching above the rows of corn on his family's farm, with his grandma on one side and his grandpa on the other, rocking him back and forth, with nothing but time.

He remembered his grandma's smile as she listened to her beloved husband tell story after story. If his grandpa noticed, he would always pause, touch her hand, and say, "I love you, honey, forever and always." His grandpa made sure to tell Thomas that once he knew he loved a woman, to never go a day without telling her. Never leave the house, fall asleep or end an argument without letting her know how he felt. No moment was too big or too small to say I love you.

Thomas began to cry with his grandpa's words echoing in his broken mind, holding his breath, and clenching his jaw to ensure no one noticed. He had done a masterful job of keeping those emotions at bay during the flight, but imagining his grandpa saying those words, was just too much.

Thomas realized he never had the chance to tell Kawai he loved her. It was the worst pain he had ever felt. He had finally found his home in her arms, and he didn't take the chance to tell her how much that meant to him. They planned their life together but didn't say the three words that every human yearns to hear. The words that keep people going, make them feel special and give each of them something to fight for.

When Lance pulled Thomas into the fight, he wished he broke loose, if only for a second, to run into her arms, give her the biggest hug, longest kiss, and tell Kawai that he loved her. Tell her she was what he would be fighting for, that no matter the distance between them, she would be the only thing on his mind—front and center, above every bullet, man, or bomb. Every strategic move, close call, and battle won would come second to his love for her. Soon enough, they'd be reunited, in each other's arms, full of love with nothing but time ahead; time to start a family, save for their dreams, and cherish every moment.

Thomas's emotions turned to anger and determination. Angry that the Japanese had taken that moment from him. Upset that the Navy pulled him hundreds of miles away to fight a war with no end in sight. And determined to say those words to her, to tell her he loved her the proper way. No matter how much he wanted to escape, return to Hawaii, find Kawai, and run away holding her hand, he couldn't. There was a job to do, a battle to prepare for, and a war to win. No one knew if Kawai was alive or dead, but the only way Thomas would find out would be to give this war everything he had.

Thomas vowed to give Kawai and the war every ounce of willpower he had from that moment on. He convinced himself, looking out into the great unknown, that she was, in fact, alive, and the first step to that becoming a reality was to claim victory and return home safe. The Navy wasn't the only thing that mattered to Thomas anymore. Kawai was it for him. She was the love of his life, the home where his heart resided, and the key to all his dreams coming true. He was a better pilot with tears running down his face and thousands of emotions in his heart than any time before.

Every soldier looks for their why. Why are they fighting the battle they are? For Thomas, as much as he wanted to avenge his brothers killed on Pearl Harbor Day, his why rested in the eyes of Kawai, and seeing her face on the day he finally told her that he loved her. Thomas found peace in his newfound mission as he drifted to sleep several hours into the flight to hell. He dreamed of what seeing Kawai would be like and how he would react at that moment. Lessons and memories of his grandparents came-and-went, before he was awoken, suddenly, by Commander Styles.

"Alright ladies, heads up and eyes open," Commander Styles demanded from the front of the plane. "We're heading to a training ground in Australia. I can't tell you where exactly, but I will tell you we will be training over the next five months to perform flawless air raids, escorts, and various missions over the Pacific. One after another."

This was music to Thomas's ears. As some wondered what all the rush and silence was about, just to train for months before any real action, he was relieved. He could prepare his mind even more for battle, write Kawai, and hear from her before his first mission.

When the squadron arrived at their destination, training ran around the clock. Strict schedules and long hours left little time for writing. Heightened anxiety about an attack on the lower-48 kept everyone on their toes. On the other hand, Thomas put stock in the five-month timeline, thinking of and writing to Kawai every chance he got.

Some of his letters were long, nearly five pages, others short notes, all written every day, until she responded. Thomas wrote about anything on his mind, going into detail about his plans for their life together, how sorry he was that he didn't stay with her that morning at the diner, and what life would be like after this was all over. He filled her in as best he could about the situation around him, even though he knew any detail would be blacked out before hitting her mailbox. To put the ideal ending to each letter, Thomas made sure Kawai knew how much he loved her and that the reason he was training for war was to fall into her arms once again.

Dear Kawai,

The wind on the deck is heavy, but I don't mind that. I can hear your voice in every gust, see your face in every crashing wave and feel your presence in the heat of the sun.

Days in the air are short, but nights on this deck are long and lonely. By now, I'm sure you're wondering why I'm still writing, but that should never cross your mind. Those two nights in your arms mean more to me than a year anywhere else. The memories I have from those hours keep me hopeful, and your necklace ensures my safety, just as you said it would.

I often stare at your initials on the wood bead, and my mind begins to race. I ponder where you might be, what you may be doing if you're safe, and if your heart feels the same as I do. I wonder what our children would be like, especially a little girl with her name filling the empty bead next to yours.

Comfort has become difficult with each passing day, but I'm managing. I can't speak much about what's happening here, but I know Lance is still not as good of a pilot as me, even if I sometimes let him think he is.

I'm rambling now, but I love you, Kawai, forever and always.

I'll never give up on us, give up on you or the stars that lead me back to you with every passing night.

Aloha Nui Loa,

Thomas

Kawai was why he stayed an extra run in the air or asked another question during a meeting. As the winter months gave birth to an anxious spring, each letter went un-answered. Hundreds had been sent, somedays more than one, and each passed without anything in return. Every soldier around him had gotten at least one letter from their family or girlfriend back home. Though receiving a letter from Pennsylvania never crossed his mind, getting one with a bright Hawaiian post-stamp was all he wished for.

Every night ended with Thomas praying to the heavens above. Not for protection from the Japanese or strength to overcome the uphill battle before him, but to receive just one letter from Kawai. He didn't care if danger was there to greet him at every turn in the air or each mission resulted in a close call, as long as he knew the woman he loved was alive. Dreams of Kawai and their future together gave way to desperate ones of a letter appearing on his pillow at day's end, with her signature on the front. Those dreams became more vivid every night, as every detail of the first word from her ran endlessly in his mind.

It would be the end of a long day in the air, at the range, or in intelligence debriefs. Thomas would begin the vision skipping an evening meal, to stumble through the makeshift front door of his room on the destroyer he had called home for months now. Lance would be fast asleep on the bunk below him, with a pillow around his head and a thin blanket. The frustration of Lance's disorganization, with clothes thrown in every direction, dirty boots lacking a shine, and upright position beneath the bed, would give way to the feeling of falling into his own sheets for the night.

Excitement would begin to build as Thomas laid down, placing his arm under the pillow as he adjusted the blanket over him, feeling the surprising touch of an envelope. Thomas would throw the pillow, backing against the wall behind him and lighting a match from Lance's stash on the nightstand beside their beds, to open a present sweeter than any toy he'd received as a child. In the smoke-filled light, a letter from Kawai confirming her health and love for Thomas appeared. His fantasy played out each night as he slept restlessly, and one brisk late-April night, Commander Styles awoke him before he reached the climax.

"Metic, Jones, get up, now," Styles shouted as he smacked the front of their beds. "You two have orders to ship out and join Admiral Fletcher to defend our position in the Coral. You're shipping out at 0500, which gives you about 20-minutes to find some damn clothes and get your asses up."

Thomas and Lance jumped anxiously to their feet, stumbling over Lance's disorganization to find any clean uniforms they could, grabbing good luck charms and mementos for the air as they rushed from the barracks. Planes were readied for Thomas, Lance, and the other "lucky" men that had stood out to Commander Styles and the rest of the Navy brass over the past months since arriving in Australia, to head straight for the Pacific War frontlines.

Thomas had caught the eye of his commanding officers since post-Pearl Harbor training had begun. His laser focus approach had become infamous at Pearl before December 7th, since then it had been taken up a notch and recognized as the gold standard in the squadron. Before the war was inevitable, Thomas's attention to detail was of obvious annoyance to those around him, especially the men assigned to work on various flight crews alongside him.

After the attack, those men who once scoffed at Thomas's techniques now envied them. Everyone in the squadron looked up to Lieutenant Metic now and did all they could to soak up his information. Those who now realized they should have been working their hardest in the months and years before the Pearl Harbor attacks were desperately attempting to gain any knowledge possible, to hopefully have a better chance of surviving. Thomas's knowledge and leadership had put him head-and-shoulders above the rest. Lance was right behind him, benefiting from his close-knit relationship with Thomas to speed up his development and reputation within the squadron, especially in the eyes of the brass.

As they rushed to the deck and into their planes, forcing them into their first combat experience of the war, Thomas was side-tracked by one of the men from his flight crew.

"Metic, Metic," the man shouted as Thomas and Lance rushed to the awaiting planes. "A letter came for you late last night; it must have fallen out of the stack as I made my rounds!"

"Kawai," Thomas whispered to himself as his eyes filled up with tears of excitement and relief.

"We don't have time, Thomas; let's go," Lance demanded as he threw a bag into the cockpit of his Fighter. "It will be here when we get back, or they'll just send it to you there."

CHAPTER 6

"Go get the chalk from the control room and throw it to me," Thomas shouted from the cockpit of his plane, cranking the engine over as the propellers began to spin, turning faster with each rotation.

"Thomas, Jesus, we have to go now. The heavies will be at our pick-up point any minute," Lance said as he watched a member of the flight crew throw the chalk up to Thomas, gear hanging from his arms, goggles and helmet already in place. "Aren't you normally the one who is on time and organized?"

"You're looking at a shining example of an American pilot, Lance," Thomas said as he stood from his cockpit, looking down on Lance as he threw the chalk. "Thank you, and seriously, I have your back up there, so watch mine."

"You already know that," Lance replied as he balled his hand into a fist, backing up slowly from Thomas's plane before running to his own.

Thomas situated himself inside the cockpit, placing the chalk against the gauges as he made sure all his equipment was in place for performance and comfort. One last adjustment of his jacket, a quick check of his first aid kit and radio before pulling his worn-out dark brown gloves over his hands and reaching once again for the chalk.

Up-and-down the deck, pilots and their crew wished on lucky stars, prayed to the heavens above, and held pictures of their loved ones tight before placing them in sight for motivation during the uncertain times ahead. Those black-and-white photos gave America's pilots the strength to win the war and secure freedom back home. Every odd beaten against better-equipped enemies, and mission completed, was done by men simply trying to get home. They all had their why, and as they strapped themselves into their flying coffins, throwing themselves into hell, that's all that ensured their safety. The training was there, intelligence in front of them and a plan in place, but the love they felt in their hearts and remembered in the glow of the faded pictures taped to their gauges was what really pulled them through.

Thomas fell in love with Kawai before the milk bought from the local market went sour. It was a whirlwind romance, and though they both had anxiety about the possibilities of war, Kawai never took the time to give Thomas a picture of herself, and he never thought to ask. They were too lost in the perfection of each other's eyes and the comfort of their touch to act on any danger ahead.

While launch time approached, Thomas pondered over the vivid memory of Kawai. All he had to look forward to was a memory he hoped never faded and one that led him straight back to her. The hope to make thousands more, keeping her close to his heart.

Her brilliant, bright smile would make anyone forget about the pain of yesterday and the anxiousness of tomorrow. Her eyes pierced his soul in a way a man only feels once in his life, the hazel-brown shade throwing Thomas's heart into his stomach. Soft, curly locks in which the moonlight danced upon, laid perfectly against her bronze skin. Her laugh was as sweet and innocent as a baby learning to speak. Everything about her, which a picture could never capture, was being painted in the mind of a terrified but focused pilot.

With the final seconds ticking by before take-off and final radio checks ringing in Thomas's ear, he reached for the chalk, eyes closed. Thomas leaned forward to a small, open space on his gauges, perfectly insight through whatever the next few hours had in store. His hand shook faster than the propellers just feet in front of his body, but Thomas stayed the course, etching "K.M." in front of him with the same hand that would eventually kill another man in the name of war. No matter how small or simple of a gesture this was, Thomas's internal confidence reached a new height as he embarked on his journey into battle.

Those two letters represented the warmness of the past, the difficulty of the present, and the hope Thomas still carried for the future. Reassurance that once this mission was over and his squadron returned victorious and all accounted for, the dreams of opening a letter from Kawai, with her health and love for him written in such beautiful and profound words, would await him. As the canopy above him shut, Thomas daydreamed of the day Kawai's initials wouldn't change, but her last name would flip from Mehelona to Metic. *Mrs. Kawai Metic.* It had a lovely ring to it.

Everything would fall into place. Their dreams and plans would assemble on the most glorious of timelines. Overdue love would be made, leading to the perfect children to carry on the legacy and retell the most farfetched stories. The first step to happiness was mustering up enough courage, strength, and confidence in his abilities to win the battle in front of him, ensuring the mission was completed and finding their safe point.

Maybe it was wishful thinking that everything Thomas wanted to happen, in the exact timeline he hoped and prayed for, would become a reality. Still, it was precisely what he needed to bolster himself as he took off, pulling his landing gear in and pealing his eyes on the horizon. Thomas led his squadron into the bright Pacific sky. There were no clouds around- nothing but open spaces to hide them from Japanese fighters.

The squadron was assigned to intercept an incoming Japanese bomber escort group. A sense of calm fell over Thomas as they approached the estimated engagement point. Light-hearted jokes filled the radio when he keyed to ask Lance if he remembered how to engage the turret. No one spoke of it, but they all were surprised they had seen no action until this point. A calm mission was even more nerve-wracking than a routine mission, especially when they all knew the danger awaiting them. Every pilot knew the Japanese subs or carriers had picked up on their position by now, but no one dared to speak of it.

"Let's get some altitude, Jones," Thomas demanded over the radio as he pulled back on the stick, climbing at an accelerated clip. "Something is up; we should have come across them by now. Let's move into what little clouds are up there and tighten up."

"10-4," Lance responded as he followed Thomas into the scarce array of clouds above them, leading a squadron of uneasy pilots.

Thomas focused on not letting his inexperience get the best of him, hoping to come across the Japanese before they flipped the narrative and took the offensive playbook straight from the American Navy's grasp. For the past four months, Thomas spent every day hoping it wasn't the eve of his first mission. The training was only comfort for him, a means to ease the heartache and give his wrist and mind a break from writing countless letters to Kawai. When the time to engage in LIVE action came, Thomas worried about performing. When that moment came, however, flying in a tight formation, brothers on each side of him, the trust Thomas felt in his abilities, and the mission at hand made him feel superhuman.

Ever since he learned of a letter finally showing up for him and Kawai's memory riding along in the form of two chalk letters and a few warm memories, Thomas felt as close to invincible as one could in their first combat experience. Call it ignorance or recklessness, but it was the place Thomas had to go to lead the men flying with him. Nervous and timid or anxious and hopeless wouldn't cut it; cocky and confident, with a touch of ignorance, was the exact recipe needed on this given day.

Just when Thomas was getting ready to lead the squadron back to base, calling the day a wash and to begin regrouping for an unknown Plan B... planes, *tons of them*, appeared just off in the distance, a few hundred feet below and to the east of Thomas and his men's position. A flashback to the last time he saw those infamous red dots painted to the side of the enemies' planes, and they were off, catching the Japanese completely by surprise, similar to how they'd hoped to engage the United States.

Thomas led the engagement of the Japanese without a second's hesitation. It had been the surest of his abilities as a pilot since the last training session before Kawai entered his life. Her memory didn't depart his mind as he swooped the squadron down and surprised the Japanese, giving them a taste of the jolt sent through each man and woman on the island of O'ahu just a few months prior; he used it as fuel for added motivation.

None of his hope for the future would become a reality if he were killed in action over the Coral Sea. Thomas wouldn't be able to live out his fantasy of opening a letter from the love of his life, reading about her health, and continued feelings for him if he were captured during the first mission he took part in. Being a prisoner of war or having a marked Cadillac pulling in front of his next-of-kin's house informing them of his death and leaving Kawai to find out secondhand couldn't happen. It wasn't going to happen that way, not this time.

With all the trust in his abilities, Thomas quickly jumped behind two enemy fighters. Lance scored the squadron's first confirmed kill of the war, nabbing a Japanese Zero straight out of the sky before the pilot could react. This only added to the hope Thomas felt aboard his plane, pushing it to max speed, following every move of the two pilots ahead of him, who surprisingly refused to split.

Bank for bank, roll to roll, Thomas followed every move, performing effortlessly with his throttle input and plane control, waiting for just the right moment to push his thumb down on the turret. With every move made, Thomas caught a glimpse of the initials on his gauges, giving him a bit more power and pushing him to finish the dogfights off on top.

Thomas remained disciplined. A touch of the turret here, push of the throttle there, and a change of direction to follow. Every move was made with precision. He knew he was at an equipment disadvantage. The Japanese Zero Fighter was one of the fastest fighter planes known to man, which meant fundamentals and heart would pay off. Who wanted it more? Who wanted to honor their country and return home to their loved ones the most? Thomas had no doubt; it was him.

Payback was on his mind. He wanted to make the Japanese understand what loss was like and how it felt to have someone repaying the fight, not laying down and surrendering. The pilot he was fighting was most certainly just like Thomas. An average guy, putting it on the line for God, country, and family, but that didn't matter. It was "him or me," in the mind of Lt. Metic. Thomas would be going home at night's end, and the man ahead of him would be in prison or a box, shipped back to Japan.

The battle wore on, stretching away from the rest. A rollercoaster it was. Up, down, and everywhere in between. Thomas had both of them hurt as Lance joined the fight, already two confirmed kills to his name and living up to the L-Ace nickname he nabbed before the war began. With sweat filling his eyelids and the fuel on his gauge reaching dangerous levels, Thomas opened the turret up, laying every ounce of American pride on the line.

One bullet after another pierced the canopy and left-wing of the Zero ahead as the pilot fled desperately to the few remaining clouds above, trying to lose Thomas in the process. Banking to his right, the pilot left his most vulnerable and damaged spot in perfect sight of Thomas and his 50-Cal'. He didn't miss. Smoke began to fill the air above, left to right. The pilot stubbornly hoped to shake Thomas, refusing to bailout over the empty sea, now miles away from the Bomber Escort Group he was assigned to.

A man Thomas had never met, who was guilty by association, perished in front of his eyes due to his actions, defending and protecting what was his. Thomas felt many emotions; he could barely speak, keying the mic for a split second. "Holy shit, Lance," Thomas said, fighting back a smile and tears, at the same time. He had never felt the way he did at this moment, but there was no time to dwell; the battle wasn't over yet.

Thomas and Lance returned to the Squadron, who had not been as lucky, losing multiple planes and a handful of men. Thomas pleaded with Lance to turn back and head home, as the Bombing Campaign they were trying to halt had turned themselves just miles from their safe point. Lance refused, and Thomas had no choice but to follow.

The two gained altitude and hoped their fuel would last as they spun in a 360-motion, flipping their P-40 nose towards the surface, coming straight down on the top of two Japanese bombers. It was time to leave a lasting mark. Taking a few fighters was a job well done, but sending a heavy into the ground would be a morale booster the whole Navy needed.

This time Thomas attached himself to Lance's six, following him, before changing direction at the last moment to stay away from on-coming fire. Lance took the front of the bomber while Thomas distracted those operating the guns, swooping below the plane, then back up, before performing a direct, punishing hit to the rear of the aircraft, destroying multiple engines and piercing a wing.

A second pass was in order, as they made sure to send a message heard all the way around the Pacific, nearly emptying their ammo and forcing the heavy into a downward free fall, with no one jumping to bailout. It was a painful end to the life of each crew member of the Japanese Bomber Team, but Thomas and Lance felt things they had never experienced in their young lives.

Relief, horror of what they had seen, and anxiety to get themselves back to the carrier filled their minds. It was almost as if they had used all of their luck up, as dozens of American pilots with whom they started the mission weren't coming home. Several planes they spent each day massaging on and flying alongside were leagues beneath the Pacific water. Men with families and the same hope for the future Thomas felt, were dead.

Though exuberant for what they had accomplished, they'd lost three fighters, a bomber, and a dozen or so men, all taken out due to their unbelievable acts of heroism. They weren't exactly sure what to feel, and the day wasn't exactly over yet, either. Poor communication with the ground and nearly empty tanks meant a dreadfully slow and anxious flight to safety. The chances of being attacked were slim but never zero, as Thomas and Lance coasted through the air, leading what was left of a dismantled and battered squadron. Everyone was silent, no chatter on the radio, just thoughts amongst themselves.

Pearl Harbor Day was the worst of Thomas's life, like thousands of others on the island and Americans back home. His pain was rooted in the tragedy of being separated from a woman he loved and their future together being put on pause. Her condition was unknown, and the pain he saw in her eyes cut deep inside, deeper than he ever knew when they were pulled from each other. Pain and tragedy were the day's theme for many on the island, but Thomas's was unique.

His pain wasn't due to direct combat experiences. Thomas and Lance never made it into the battle or even assisted in putting up some defense. Every corner they turned led to a dead end, and their call to action was giving blood, holding the hand of the wounded, and searching for those missing in action: no direct combat, dogfight gone wrong, or bomb landing beside them to awaken their sleeping bodies.

Many of the other pilots, nursing their planes home in silence, were numbed to the thought of combat. Pearl Harbor and their experiences of getting dominated by the Japanese had prepared their minds for what they just went through before it ever happened. This wasn't new to them. Thomas had spent the last four months figuring out how to get back to Kawai and convincing himself she was alive. Those around him were training desperately to make sure they were more prepared to fight and never experienced the horror of an attack like Pearl Harbor again.

Thomas had just been through his first combat mission, dogfight and now running on fumes to make it to safety in one piece. Fuel and the chances of the propellers on his plane locking up never crossed his mind. His performance, dogfights won, and the strategic call he made to gain altitude before engaging the Japanese Bomber Escort Group, which directly led to the mission's success, didn't either. Those lost? Selfishly, all Thomas could think about was the fact he had made it through the battle, all limbs attached and no bullet holes in his canopy, checking off the first of what he hoped were only a few on a short list of close calls in the sky between himself and being reunited with Kawai.

He looked forward to debriefs, down-time with the squadron, and even prayers for those lost because it meant he was out of harm's way. Of course, he hurt for the brothers left behind, but letting his mind go to that point, was the most dangerous thing he could do. From discussions after long training sessions with those who came before him and the old-timers who fought in The Great War, Thomas had formed an ability to move on from the men's deaths around him. Whether it was those lost on December 7th or just minutes prior, Thomas had an uncanny ability to understand what had taken place, deal with it quickly and file those feelings as far back into his memory bank as mentally possible.

With their safe point appearing on the horizon, relief and an anxious pit of butterflies filled Thomas's stomach. He couldn't wait to get into his bed and open the letter waiting for him. Thomas could only imagine the good news waiting as he rushed through post-mission debriefs and prayer for those left behind.

Nothing would stand between Thomas, that sheet of thin paper, and the beautiful rows of ink he hoped were there. Kawai would assure him of her health, her family's health, and how things were back in Hawaii. She would make sure he knew she would be waiting for him when he returned, no matter how long it took, and their plans for the future would happen just as they planned. Most of all, Kawai would say those three-words Thomas ended each of his letters with. The eight letters, perfectly aligned, would make all the tears shed, the anxiety felt, and the fatigue endured worth it. Seeing Kawai tell Thomas that she loved him was what he knew he needed to pass the time, however long it took until he laid his eyes on her again and felt her soft touch. Knowing Kawai was alive and that she loved him just as much as he loved her would make every early morning less painful, each mission easier to prepare for, and passing moment without her by his side faster.

Thomas entered his room alone, rushing to get away from the rest of the squadron and buy some alone time. Weeding through Lance's left disorganization, he quickly untucked his even sheets and placed a stack of perfectly folded clothes on the stand beside his pillow. Next came the pillow itself, thrown to the side, making his way to the letter.

The hope for what the letter held was higher than the first time his lips met Kawai's. Thomas's heart beat out of his chest faster than the first time they made love. Butterflies thicker than trying to speak to her for the first time and anxiety richer than at any point during the mission he had just completed. Many months, hundreds of days, and thousands of hours had led to this.

His heart sank faster than any destroyer had during the war as he grabbed the letter and read the mailing address: John Richards, Reading, PA. A name Thomas hadn't seen or heard in over a decade was one he could live without ever hearing again, especially at this moment.

Seeing Kawai's name and a Hawaiian address was all he wanted. Not holding her, kissing her, or even seeing her, was fine; he could find ways to deal with that and had, but not knowing if she loved him or even if she was alive, cut like a thousand knives. This feeling was more profound than Thomas had ever felt. Deeper than the last time he saw his grandparents, attended their funeral or the morning of December 7th, when he was ripped from Kawai's arms.

John Richards was an old friend, a neighbor who had lived beside Thomas's grandparents' house. John wrote to check up on Thomas after seeing his name in a newspaper article of local heroes fighting the good fight somewhere in the Pacific for Roosevelt and Uncle Sam. There was nothing good about the battle going on in Thomas's head. He had waited hours, an entire mission, not to mention dozens of lonely days, with a false sense of wonder if that could be the one he finally received the long-awaited letter.

Thomas's mind scrambled like burnt eggs in a skillet. Positivity was an afterthought as he ripped the letter in half, crumbling it up until it was in a mangled ball on the floor, adding to the mess beside Lance's bed. He had locked in all day in the air, looking forward to this moment. Each move he had, was played out in front of her initials riding along in front of him. Every shot taken, move made, and plane taken down was done effortlessly, hoping his day would end with being reassured of Kawai's feelings and safety, at last.

Instead, Thomas was left to grab a flask at the bottom of a bag under his bed and find somewhere else but that room and in that bed to sit in his sorrow. He settled for the carrier's stern, taking them to begin training again and wait for orders on their next mission.

The air was thin on this mild May evening in the middle of the Pacific. A thin line of sunlight on the horizon remained as Thomas leaned against the railing, wondering where she might be and what she might be doing. Fighting back emotions had become a daily hobby of sorts for Thomas, and he wasn't alone in that regard. Many of his squad-mates were missing home or already had demons of past combat. All of them seemed to push those feelings as far down as possible, and everyone aboard the carrier was doing just that, as Thomas could hear the ongoing party from where he was standing.

He didn't blame them for celebrating, the mission was a success, and for those select few pounding shots, they were alive and lucky for it. Of course, there was the loss, but that was part of everyday life in the Pacific. There was a high chance that on the runway before takeoff, the man in front of you, behind you, or yourself wouldn't be landing the same plane, with the same limbs and heartbeat, at day's end. That was life in the Navy, but Thomas was over keeping those emotions in check.

Tears began to roll down both cheeks as anger set in. Thomas squeezed the flask in his hands so hard it began to slip. A flask his father had given him the day he enlisted in the Navy, never opened, with the same life-altering substance as it had when Mr. Metic handed it to his son. Thomas had never had a sip of alcohol, but he already knew he was an addict, and if he started now, there was no telling if and when he would stop. He had seen first-hand what the poison in that flask does to people. It aided in medicating his dad each night while also subscribing his family to a life of struggle, hunger, and fear.

He was sure the 100-proof liquid could ease his pain, but he also had plenty of proof of what the aftermath would hold. Opening the flask, smelling the alcohol inside, and leaning it back for a much-needed sip, Thomas decided against it. Dumping every last drop over the railing and throwing the flask as far into the Pacific as he could muster.

No medication or liquid courage, just time to sit in pain. Thomas fell to his knees and backed against the railing, crying harder than the day he shoveled dirt on his grandpa's coffin or saw his dad lay a hand on his mom. This was the lowest point of Thomas's life. Hope, confidence, and reasons to stay positive were all he could think about since meeting the woman he was meant to love, even after departing from her.

Kawai never did ask him why he didn't pour a glass of wine for himself on their second night together, and though a million lessons learned, moments endured, and horrific scenes shot through his mind, her sweet touch of understanding stuck out. She must have figured he didn't like wine and bought it only because of her dream or wanted to be respectful; whatever it was, she never asked or gave him a hard time for not taking a sip. From his teens to his early days in the military and bunking with Lance, that's all those his age would do; make fun of his lack of drinking and wonder why he never tried to fit in. Kawai didn't care; what he presented her, on the surface, was good enough.

Of course, the past months had been hard, but the hope he remembered seeing in her eyes or the memories of Kawai making all the worry he felt disappear always brought him something to look forward to. At this moment, crying on the hard floor of a ship in the middle of the ocean, with his peers partying until everything went black as a backdrop, there was nothing to look forward to.

Not even the necklace Kawai gave Thomas just moments before the attack could bring him happiness. He pulled the old shop rag out of his pocket, unfolding it until the brown pearl and the initials that accompanied it so effortlessly were in full sight. Thomas did everything he could to look at the necklace as little as possible, not even opening it as he sat on the runway waiting for launch that morning. It smelled like her, and each time he unwrapped the rag, picked it up, and held it close to him, that smell dissipated just a little more.

'*She was right about the necklace,*' Thomas thought as he locked his hands, palms open with the rag against his skin and necklace arranged on top. It had kept him safe, even helping him perform better than his wildest expectations. The brown stone, which glowed nearly as beautiful as her eyes, could bring him many things. Memories of her, scents of her perfume, and even close to the feeling of her skin against his. Vivid images of the stars aligned and moonlight dancing through her hair, in the moments their love was formed, raced through his mind each time he held the piece of Kawai's family history. What it couldn't do was bring him her, show him her safety or tell him her love.

The noise of the partying tapered with Thomas still alone on the ground as the air became brisk, with a cloudy, grim sky above. There were no stars to watch or moonlight for comfort. Open seas and darkness for as far as the eye could see. The quietness made Thomas feel more alone by the second and his internal dialogue became deafening.

He knew he couldn't stay out all night but realized that he wouldn't be the same when the new day began. There wouldn't be hope that a letter from the most gorgeous woman in Hawaii would be handed to him. No motivation to train harder or succeed in the air. To Thomas, as he walked back to his room, head down, hoping to avoid any straggling drunken pilots or those assigned to night watch, every day from here on out was a simple math equation.

There were 24-hours in a day; 6-8 would be for sleeping, which became the only thing to look forward to. The other 16 would be spent going through the motions, showing enough commitment, and doing what he had to do not to be asked questions. His performance in the air no longer mattered. Missions won were a second thought. Every pilot around him had the same opportunities as he did to fly their planes and develop their skills, so their safety was now an afterthought.

Kawai was his purpose. Making his way back to Hawaii and laying his eyes on her was all that mattered. Those feelings and dreams were dashed. He began the day as she would have hoped, positive, confident, and ready. The night ended worse than she ever could have imagined. Her necklace had protected him physically, but nothing short of her word could save him emotionally.

CHAPTER 7

Six months had passed since the Battle of the Coral Sea, but the battle between Thomas's ears remained. With the holidays right around the corner and no clear end to the War in the Pacific, or World War II in general, every day had the same schedule. Up at 0600, breakfast, debriefs, training, lunch, more training, cleaning duty, dinner, and bed. Same order, from sun-up, to sun-down, as the day before, the mindset Thomas carried remained consistent.

No one knew when and if they would return to battle again. They heard stories of battles being won and ground gained all around them, but no one knew what was next. Each man could be sent home tomorrow or have a week-long mission thrown on their lap with no warning. The squadron had performed various bomber escorts, mostly from safe-point to safe-point, with little interaction with the enemy. Clean sailing, no loss, and little stress meant a light-hearted group and close-nit squadron, but none of that interested Thomas. Everyone around him knew of his personality: all business, all the time. No time for play remained after finding the letter from John Richards, but the microfocus on his job had left.

No longer did Thomas beat the rest of the squadron to the debrief room. He wasn't the first on the flight deck or runway, helping his crew make final checks before takeoff and joking around to keep things light. Making sure those he was assigned to lead's heads were in the game used to be high on his priority list; now, it didn't cross his mind.

Training, meetings, patrols, or the latest rumor of a mission, didn't matter to Thomas or change his mood. He was there when he had to be, but not a minute sooner or later. Talking with the men or chopping it up with them didn't happen; in when he was assigned to be, gone when his commitment time elapsed.

The week before Christmas 1942, Thomas was called into a meeting with Commander Styles and Lance, where the Commander made it clear that Lance would be leading the men in the air. No one trusted Thomas any longer to go the extra mile or do what it took to bring as many of them home, when the time came, as they had before. During the Battle of the Coral Sea, you couldn't find one man who didn't trust Thomas or wouldn't fly with him into whatever situation they had to. Now, there wasn't one pilot, even Lance, who would follow Thomas to the lunchroom, let alone into a mission that could bring their final breath.

Thomas didn't have the energy to explain where his mind was or why he had changed his leadership style so suddenly. The Navy wouldn't care to hear his excuses, anyhow; there was a war, and, in their eyes, it didn't matter what anyone was going through upstairs; they needed to be focused on the task at hand.

He had lost his why. Thomas and the rest of his squadron had been stationed in Australia for over a year. Each man around him had received hundreds of letters from home. Thomas had received one from a man he barely remembered, telling him about an article he had seen in the newspaper. In his mind, there was no reason to keep fighting, and going through the motions was what he had to do to avoid issues with the brass. Weather the storm until the war was over, and he could return to Hawaii to find out exactly what had happened to the love of his life.

Christmas brought Thomas a new set of challenges as the squadron met for drinks and a meal. Like he always did, Thomas arrived late, taking water instead of whiskey and keeping quiet as the rest of the men told stories of women from their past and dreams for the future. The men spoke about what they would be doing when they returned home and, in most cases, who they would be doing. This meal was no different in that aspect, as conversations like these were the new normal until Lance broke from the norm, hoping to break Thomas's radio silence.

"I want to propose a toast," Lance said as he stumbled to his feet, standing on his chair, pointing his glass towards Thomas. "To the United States Navy, Commander Styles, and President Roosevelt for finally coming to their senses to realize who should be leading you all into battle."

"You're a real hero, Jones," Thomas said as he stood up and walked away from the table.

"Look here, boys, the great Lt. Metic," Lance shouted as he jumped from his chair, walking in Thomas's direction. "He's off to chase ghosts."

"Be careful, Jones," Thomas said as he stopped in his tracks and turned to Lance. "You're drunk and don't have the slightest clue what's coming out of your mouth."

"The truth," Lance said as he threw his drink down, walking up to Thomas. "That's the truth,

Thomas. You're chasing something that's no longer there. I have friends still stationed at Pearl, we all do, and we've all heard the stories. Dozens of locals died when the torpedoes rolled in, and it all happened exactly where you two were that morning and where you left her. She's dead, Thomas, and if she isn't, she's sleeping with another fly boy from another squadron-"

Thomas swung before Lance could finish his speech, landing a shot directly above his eye. Lance returned the favor, tackling Thomas and bringing them onto the wood floor below. The scrap between the two former friends lasted only seconds before the rest of the men broke them up.

"You're the reason I left her," Thomas shouted as he was being restrained.

"We had a job to do then, just like we do now," Lance responded in a deep, quiet voice in-between breaths. "Move on before you get one of us killed!"

Thomas's Christmas night ended in Commander Styles's office, once again, this time with a bag of ice, wrapped in a cloth, held against the side of his head. He was ashamed and wished the past six months hadn't happened. Thomas wished he wouldn't have put so much stock into that one letter and just did what he had to do, to find the motivation to keep going and lead his men.

Maybe Lance was right. For all Thomas or anyone else knew, Kawai was dead or had moved on with someone else, but there was no way of knowing. As Thomas waited for Commander Styles to start speaking, he contemplated how to let her go, move on, and do his job. She was why he fought so hard and focused so sharply in the Coral. Moving on and finding other reasons to fight, train hard and study as he had before that mission wasn't easily found, and even in his lowest moment, he struggled to locate them.

"Lt. Metic, I used to look up to you," Commander Styles began, with his hands folded against the desk. "Men like you, even before Pearl, made me believe that we had a fighting chance in this war. It made me think we could take on the Japanese, Germans, and even the devil himself. When you were first tested, you performed above the call of duty. Leading your men and making decisions that saved yourself and their lives and helped turn the momentum in this war. Now, I'm not going to even begin to understand why your focus has changed so much since then, but I believe I owe you the truth, man-to-man, even if those around me believe it's the wrong decision."

The Commander paused as he reached to the side of his desk, opening a drawer at the bottom, bringing a stack of envelopes to the surface.

"I believe these are letters you have written a local woman near Pearl," Commander Styles said as he walked around his desk and handed them to Thomas before leaning against it and facing him. "Lt. Jones said you never received any letters back from her, which may be why you've been the way you have."

"Yes, sir," Thomas said as he tried to understand. "I just wanted to know if she was alive."

"Son, the Navy never mailed those letters," Styles said quietly. "Washington believes there may be locals being friendly with the Japanese, and until they can clear those worries, we can't authorize any communication between enlisted military personnel and civilians on the island of O'ahu. Especially not pilots' engaging in this war, like yourself. Your feet are too close to the fire, and our position in the Pacific is too vulnerable."

Every ounce of Thomas's being wanted to plead with Commander Styles to understand what he was going through. He wished he could convince the Commander to send those letters personally or help him find out if Kawai were alive or dead. If he knew that, Thomas could rationalize giving everything to the rest of the war. He would either be fighting to get home to her or fighting in her honor, to return home and build the dreams they talked about, with the waves crashing into their feet.

Even in the state he was in, Thomas realized that would be selfish of him, thanking the Commander for his time, assuring him he would be better moving forward and exiting his office. The military was up to their eyes in notifying the next of kin, with death certificates from thousands of American soldiers, all over the world. Convincing them to help him determine the well-being of a local Hawaiian woman didn't stand a chance, no matter how unfair Thomas viewed the situation.

Learning of the Navy's circumstances and their interference with his possible communication with Kawai was hard, but there was light at the end of the tunnel. She was no longer presumed dead or moved on with someone else. Kawai could be in love with Thomas, just as much as he was with her, miss him at the level he did her, and dream about the future they could build together when she slept, as he did every night. They just couldn't tell each other those things, which was a harsh reality, but one Thomas had to find a way to accept.

Strangely, as he laid his head down against the pillow to put a period on an eventful Christmas Day, Thomas had found the closure he was searching for. The pain of not knowing if she was alive remained, but the hope for the future had returned. If Kawai were alive, Thomas knew he wouldn't ever find out for sure until he laid his eyes on her; she was most likely waiting on him, just as he was her. The only way he would find out was to get himself back to her in one piece.

The squadron continued routine escorts and patrols over the next several weeks and months. Thomas did his best to make up for lost time, returning to his routine pre-Battle of the Coral Sea, hoping to win over the men to his right and left. Getting to the debrief room thirty minutes before everyone else, engaging with the intelligence being put forth, helping to clean up after meals, anything to show his commitment. During nights when the squadron would let loose, Thomas made sure to stay the entire time, never drinking but always staying entuned with the conversation and hoping to show each man that they could trust him and count on him again.

It was a long road and as the Summer of 1943 came and the intelligence of another big mission came forth, Thomas was sure of his abilities but unsure if those around him trusted his leadership and what he had to say. Lance was now the Squad Leader in the air, but Thomas questioned if that was the right decision.

During many patrols and escorts, Lance had been skittish in his calls, asking for opinions of those around him, even the most inexperienced of pilots, before finally deciding what should be done. Thomas remained silent but worried that when the chips were down and everything was on the line, Lance wouldn't be able to make the split-second decision that saved each of their lives.

All Thomas could do was his job. Focus on what he could control and rebuild the bridges he had nearly burned the months before Christmas. Hot summer days and uncertainty of when the mission rumored for weeks would take place built frustration within the men around Thomas, especially Lance. Thomas had been roommates with Lance for as long as they could remember, and he had never seen him this way. Every fourth of July, before the war, their squadron would get together and celebrate the birthday of the country they were defending. This year brought a new set of circumstances to be thankful for and celebrate. The freedom of the United States was being tested. Men like Thomas and Lance were assigned to defend it, and that brought a world of pressure, pressure Lance was struggling to deal with.

With celebrations raging on, hot dogs being eaten, and brews tipped, they finally got the word they had been waiting on. The squadron, led by Lance and Thomas, would be flying with the B-24 Liberators from Midway to Wake Island. The mission was simple: bomb the Japanese, leave a mark, send a message, and get out.

Momentum in the Pacific was with the Americans, and as the war wore on, many hoped they might be inching closer to victory with each successful mission. Getting the Liberators from Midway to Wake, and their safe point, with minimal loss, could mean a significant advancement and a chance to be home by Christmas possibly. This news meant an opportunity to Thomas and the rest of the roaring room. Maybe, just maybe, he would be back in Kawai's arms before the calendar hit 1944. He envisioned the feeling of her lips on Christmas morning, her smile and glossy eyes from a gift on Valentine's Day, and the breathtaking view of her beach attire come Spring.

Thomas forced himself to view this risky mission as nothing short of a once-in-a-lifetime chance. The possibilities and benefits of success, which came from an even higher amount of focus and effort than ever, were exciting for everyone but their squad leader. Lance took a big swig of his beer and dashed out of the room without notice from most. Thomas followed him, hoping to help his old friend through the anxiety that he once had. Kawai had kept the anxious feelings of leading men into battle at a minimum for Thomas, as his worrying focused primarily on returning home to her. Leading those around him and making the right decisions was just what had to be done; it came second nature. Lance wasn't so lucky; nothing outside of flying his plane on the limit and talking to women came easy to him, especially not leading.

After walking up to their room, checking the flight deck and debrief room, Thomas finally found Lance. He sat with a pen-and-paper and a beer on each side of his folding chair, overlooking the water.

"I never took you as much of an artist," Thomas said as he pulled up a chair to sit beside Lance.

"You know I've yet to send a letter home to my folks?" Lance said as he grabbed a tossed the paper on the deck and pen into the crashing water below. "For all they know, I'm floating in the Pacific, just like that stupid pen."

"Then write them," Thomas said with a laugh. "Pretty simple."

"And tell them what?" Lance asked as he turned to Thomas. "That I can't be sure of myself enough to lead my men."

"You're not up there alone, Lance," Thomas said quietly. "Use those around you and their strengths but be sure of your intelligence enough to make decisions quickly. During training and even the safest of patrols, you're too timid in decision-making. These men need a confident voice in their ear when all hell breaks loose, and hell may be the backdrop of this entire mission."

"Who are you to give me advice?" Lance asked as he cracked open another beer. "You were MIA for months. Didn't have a care in the world, especially not for this squadron or the war effort."

"I could sit here and spew bullshit for hours and still help you more than what you're finding in that can," Thomas responded sternly. "I've made my share of mistakes, but the last mission we were a part of required a quick decision and dogfights; I was the lead. My call got us all home; remember that and respect that."

"I'll respect you once you forget about that girl and focus on this squadron," Lance said with a shrug and wink. "Plus, I'm not your pops, so don't worry about my drinking. I'll be ready when it matters."

"Whatever you say, sweetheart," Thomas said as he stood up to walk away, trying to hold back his building frustration. "I'll let those comments go, and from the looks of it, I'll be the one leading us in the sky when it matters. Just get your ass to the flight deck. We'll see who the men turn to when their life is at stake."

Thomas walked away without another word, hearing the tipping of the can and crashing of liquid as Lance took drink after drink. He knew everything Lance was saying came from his own doubt about what the future may hold, but that didn't stop the anger. If there was anyone that knew of the pain Thomas must feel, carrying around the unknown of Kawai's condition, it was Lance. Thomas had been away from the woman he loved for nearly two years. A woman he barely knew, and the universe took from his arms, with only a few memories to fall back on. Lance was the person who greeted Thomas when the events of December 7th, 1941, were beginning. He saw the fear and desperation in Kawai's eyes as he pulled Thomas from his arms.

Lance slept every night in a bed just feet away from Thomas, watching him write letter after letter with no response. Prayers, sleepless nights, and fatigued mornings took place with Lance nearby. Every man in the squadron had demons and trauma they were fighting through, worries about what may come next and growing hopelessness of when they may see their loved ones again, but it was different for them.

Every other man could write the woman he loved, check on her, read the love she had for him and look at her picture before each mission. They never had to convince themselves of what their wife or girlfriend looked like, remind themselves of how she felt, or wonder if she was alive. Lance knew that and still chose to ride Thomas about it daily until the two barely spoke.

In the months before their duel on Christmas and into their spat, sitting in chairs over-looking the Pacific, Lance's writing habits, or lack thereof, had become irritating to Thomas. Every night before Christmas, attempting to sleep and each morning when he woke before the sun, Thomas dreamt and prayed for a letter from Kawai, which never came. Those same nights, Lance stumbled to bed and awoke with a cockiness of what his time in the air that day would entail, never picking up a pen. He had every chance to write home, with a guarantee of a response from any woman he may want to contact or his big family dying to hear from him, but he never did.

As Thomas spent the last days leading up to launch, writing letters to Kawai that would never be sent, he wondered about Lance's family. Each night, Thomas had used this time to fabricate hope in his words. What would she think, say, or do in his situation? How would she react if she knew her best friend, turned stranger, was worried but decided to hold it all in? Kawai was as family oriented as they came and would never stand for Lance not writing his kin back home.

Before he knew it, Thomas had written over a page asking Kawai, in a letter she may never see, how to handle Lance's relationship. He knew they would never talk about their issues. Pilots in the squadron drank their problems away or, in Thomas's case, wrote to what had become, to many, a fictional character. Any problems they had with each other were solved, in the air, when they had no choice but to have each other's back. When the situation meant life or death, the love that remained, deep down, would come out, and after, it would be as if no problems ever existed. Thomas figured that would be the case with Lance. Maybe hopeful but necessary, he closed his notepad and laid down, facing the wall he had spent many hours staring at.

The future was unknown, which had become the norm for Thomas and the men that lay in beds all over the destroyer. No one knew what tomorrow held or the weeks, months, and even years that followed. He wondered where Kawai was, like many evenings. If her beautiful eyes still got lost in the sunset, or the thoughts of her dreams brought a tear to them like they did when she shared them with Thomas. Believing she was alive and everything she wanted stayed in motion without Thomas there, had become therapy for him. Maybe she was somewhere just like he was, worrying about the man she still loved, holding on to the hope of seeing him again.

Thomas found comfort in thoughts of Kawai writing letters to him, expressing her love, and assuring their future. He selfishly hoped she missed him as much as he did her. It was all that remained to get him through the day and the battles on the horizon. Tomorrow wouldn't bring her beautiful eyes to his, but it meant one more day closer to them being reunited. They would grow old together. It didn't matter how slim the possibilities or odds of that happening may be, as the hell around Thomas grew closer. He believed that their Golden Years would be spent wrapped together in a blanket on the beach, reading letters from another life, one that built the bond and loyalty they now enjoyed. That fairytale, made with each word, memory, and dream, would become a reality, even if only in Thomas's mind. That was now the difference between life and death for him. The hope of a future with the woman he loved, no matter how farfetched or far away it may be.

The anxiety of a mission never changed. Whether the intel was good or not, chances of returning in one piece were high or low, the routine and thoughts that crossed Thomas's mind as he sat in the cockpit, readying to launch, remained the same.

He would arrive early, help the crew go over their checklist, perform any last maintenance needed, and climb in his plane before other pilots were even dressed for battle. He'd wipe away what was left of Kawai's faded initials at the bottom of his dashboard, rewriting them as clearly as his shaken hands would allow. He'd pray on the heavens above for a safe mission before closing his eyes, crossing his arms, and forcing himself to find a good memory of Kawai to pass the time until he fired his plane.

Kawai loved to talk about the hope she found in nature as a little girl. Hawaii was rich in nature and her people's connection to it, which attracted her from a young age. Like everyone lucky enough to be born on the islands, she was a child of the land. The universe, land, and sea were at the root of what it meant to be a young girl from O'ahu. Kawai and Thomas only spent a few days together before the world's circumstances forced them apart, but she opened Thomas's eyes to a world he never knew.

Hawaiian culture comes from the nature surrounding its people, but it's much deeper than soil, the sun that warms it, or the water that grows it. Kawai spent many nights with her mother, bright-eyed over stories of the beginning of time in Hawaii, when humankind and the nature that fed, clothed, and housed them, were one. Isolation meant a dependence on what was grown and found around them more than anywhere else in the world.

"Everything around us makes us who we are," Kawai would say, staring at the stars with the moonlight dancing in her eyes. "Each of those stars has a special meaning, something that gives us hope, reminds us of those who came before and what the future holds. I was born from everything you see around us. The food we learned to grow, an ocean that gave us the tools and guidance, sun that kissed our skin and warmed everything. Every time I feel lost, I just lay in the grass or sand, look up and find the hope of those who came-"

"Fire it up, Metic," a voice interrupted on the radio. "Five minutes to launch."

Showtime.

Thomas's heart beat through his chest as his Squadron's escort approached their target. Any moment now, they could be swarmed by Japanese fighters. There was nothing but ocean water ahead as they searched for coastline- Wake Island, their target, and a sleeping beast.

"Tighten up, boys," Lance said as he broke radio silence. "We're a few miles out, then it's bombs away and bust ass home."

Bombs scattered the skies below Thomas as he focused ahead, looking for any threat that could be looming. Lance celebrated over the radio as target after target exploded, and smoke began pouring from buildings, planes, and equipment on the ground. The Japanese seemed to be on their heels and unprepared for what had hit them.

"Watch your six," Thomas interrupted as they cleared Wake and began the voyage to safety. "No planes left the ground; they could be waiting on us."

"I'll lead the damn squad, Metic," Lance said sternly. "You just sit back and pray on your lucky stars that Commander Styles gave me the lead. Because of my fine flying and leadership, you'll get to go back to base and write another letter that will never even be sent out."

Fighters filled the skies below them as they cleared an area of clouds. Thomas was right. Quick as lightning, the squadron jumped into action, vowing to protect the bombers who had nabbed a successful mission. Thomas and Lance picked off fighters one by one, with the circumstances around them providing the lucky star they needed for success. They had the bead on every fighter, an element of surprise like their first combat experience together, as they dropped altitude right onto their heads. Quick work was made, as Lance tallied two more shot-down fighters, and Thomas led the Squadron with four confirmed kills.

"Look out for those flaks," Lance demanded as the squadron regrouped around the bombers after a successful defense of their position. "Let's get these heavies into the scoop and their safe zone. Helluva job, boys, they're going to be talking about this victory to Roosevelt's office."

Just as Lance finished his victory speech, anti-aircraft fire filled the skies around him, Thomas, and the men they were attempting to lead.

"We need to get higher!" Thomas said with desperation as the black smoke from the flaks grew thicker by the second, and American fighters scrambled for any cover they could find.

No warning, plan, or protection. Japanese gunmen lit up the sky with shots that could tear a hole through the strongest of exteriors. The loss was almost instant, as American planes and pilots who thought they were home free fell hopelessly from the Pacific sky. Thomas took a deep breath, one last look, and kiss to her initials, and he was off. A quick upward motion on the stick, and gone from the bombers he went, hoping to aid in nursing any mangled planes home that he could find.

Fading sunlight and thick smoke painted the sky. Horror overshadowed any hope found in it as Thomas manhandled his underdog plane. Flak fire grew stronger with every passing mile. Heart had returned him home before, but this time things were different.

Lances' unwillingness to move from his egotistical personality meant nothing to Thomas now, as he dipped in and out of any cloud he could find. Left to right, up and down, Thomas moved his plane swiftly in any direction that he thought would shake the darkening smoke around him. All that mattered was finding a man he signed up to protect. The situation around him had become dire as the Japanese ground fire became almost too powerful to fly through or attempt to fly above. Losses piled up by the second, the idea of giving up and high tailing his way to a safe point, hoping Lance and the others would do the same, crossed Thomas's mind. Just as he throttled up to get out of dodge, Thomas spotted a trailing plane out of the corner of his eye, black smoke following it with each degree of altitude lost.

"Pull up, pull up," Thomas replied as he flew above the ailing plane to decipher who it may be.

"I can't; there's fluid everywhere!" Lance said from the riddled cockpit.

"Lance, listen to me," Thomas said, keeping his voice calm. "The only way you'll survive is pulling that stick back and banking this plane into the clouds. We don't have much time, and there are more flaks around us that could finish the both of us off."

"Get your ass out of here!" Lance said with distress.

"If you go, I'm going with you, so pull the stick back now!" Thomas shouted.

"I'm trying; it won't go anywhere," Lance cried. "It's over for me!"

Just as Thomas keyed the radio to continue trying to help his friend to safety, one last flak pierced Lance's plane, causing a massive fire ball and emptiness in Thomas's stomach. Tears filled his eyes as he screamed for help from above. Lance was gone, and the success of the mission no longer mattered. No glory was to be had, and even if the rest of his months in Pacific were spent manning a beach amusement park ride, Lance was gone. None of his medals, confirmed kills, or missions led could save him from the inevitable or return him home to the life he left behind.

Luck that never came was all Lance Jones needed. He would fly his plane to a safe point, brag about his leadership, and live to fight another day. Just a bit of luck, and Lance would be joining Thomas with a story to tell their grandkids of the day they cheated death and moved the war effort forward. That day, as an older man, rocking along with a grandchild on both knees, sipping lemonade, would never come for Lance. Vows, anxious moments in the waiting room as his kids were being born, or even homecomings at the end of the war, weren't in God's plan for the Lieutenant.

A miracle ending wasn't meant to be. Glory for either pilot didn't make the plot. Lance's plane blew to pieces in a ball of flames before he could receive any pat on the back. What was left of his disintegrated plane smashed into the ocean and sprinkled across territory occupied by the very men who took his life. Lance's war story ended on July 8th, 1943.

Like thousands of sailors, soldiers, and pilots, Lance never got the chance to live up to his full potential. Coming of age, from chasing nurses to trying to pause the hourglass of love, never came to fruition for him. Changing from an egotistic pilot to teaching his children to be humble was no longer possible. Holding grudges against the only friend the Navy had brought him to have a beer on the anniversary of Pearl Harbor every December wasn't in the cards of life for Lance Jones. He died serving his country and leading his men, never writing home, and leaving many wondering how he felt about them or his time spent alongside them.

Thomas flew through the thick smoke that cost Lance his life, getting to him as fast as possible but coming up short. Tears fell as he flew home. It was all over. From the first time he set foot on the Pearl Harbor soil, it wasn't Kawai who greeted him; it was Lance. It wasn't his grandparents or parents who convinced him to go out the night he first laid his eyes on the woman of his dream; that would be Lt. Jones. The man who he hated most days but loved every day. A pilot who, deep down, he wished he had the guts of and who he envied for living every single day as if it were his last.

Touching down at the base, safe and sound, Thomas wondered what was going through his friend's mind as he took his last breath. Was it his family he never wrote to back home, a girl he was too proud to confess his love for, or his best friend, whom he died never mending things with? With the engine turned off, Thomas just sat in silence. What was left of a day in hell peeked between the planes in front of him and flag poles in the distance. Thomas reached for the necklace Kawai had given him what seemed like a decade ago. Her smell still hit his nose like a freshly baked pie in his grandma's kitchen. Warmth and comfort were emotions he expected and yearned to feel each time the scent of her perfume and skin reached his nose, but this time they weren't there.

No scent, memory, or letter written would heal the pain Thomas felt in his soul. The rest of the beaten-up Squadron that had made it home were in the debriefing room as he struggled to exit the plane. Just minutes before, his best friend's body crashed into the ocean, and his spirit left the earth, for a forever home with God. Thomas had ended the mission with four new confirmed kills protecting the bombers as they succeeded in their mission at Wake Island. Four new red dots on white backgrounds. A handful of recent aerial victories added to his resume, with medals and ribbons sure to follow.

"I heard you took down four," Commander Styles said as he jumped on the wing to talk to Thomas. "That makes you an Ace, son."

"He was the real Ace, sir," Thomas said, pointing to the sky, as his arms still shook from the horror left behind. "Just too bad he never got the chance to become an Ace in life."

CHAPTER 8

High winds crashed ole glory against the pole that elegantly held firm as she swayed. A Pacific Plover flew from the pole to the stern railing of the destroyer cutting through the Pacific Ocean to yet another unknown destination. Thomas watched the bird closely as it stretched its beautiful wings aloft, seemingly performing for him and him alone. He sat in the same chair Lance did months prior, with a six-pack of his favorite beer and a pad awaiting Thomas's latest letter to the love he missed so dearly.

Thomas watched the bird for hours as the holidays and another year of survival were celebrated in the background. He had named the Plover Hope, as its rich bronze-brownish wings and eyes reminded him of Kawai and the presence she carried in his heart. The beauty took flight with ease, dipping in and out of Thomas's sight, like how Kawai let herself fall into the ocean, moving with the waves as if she was one with the water. Hope resembled the comfort he found on those fateful December evenings, staring into her eyes, even as she spoke emotionally about the possibilities of impending war.

Two years had passed since the last time he saw her perfect sun-kissed skin and glowing smile. Her memory was beginning to fade, just slightly, as Thomas struggled to remember every detail. He used to be able to recount, effortlessly, the tilt of her smile. Ever since the horror of the hot July day when Lance was killed just off the coast of Wake Island, his mind had been all over the place.

Pain was nothing new to Thomas. The past two years were filled with it, but the feelings had become overwhelming since Lance was killed. Every sailor, pilot, nurse... even those who prepared the meals were expected to keep going, one boot and bullet in front of the other. Moving forward and going through the motions could be the theme of Thomas's life. From the trauma of his childhood to his whirlwind romance, Kawai being taken from him and losing his best friend without patching things up had pushed Thomas to the edge. He knew all too well what disappointment felt like.

Regret was a feeling Thomas wasn't used to. When his grandparents died, he was too young to fill his mind with what-ifs. There was nothing his teenage mind could do to change the tides of his parent's marriage and the years of adulthood in the Navy were a breeze for him. Once Kawai came into his life and the war began, each event brought a new sense of regret. Was he doing everything he could to reach her, honor her and keep her memory from slipping away? Could he do more to impact the war effort, to return to her arms quicker? What if he never left her? Day after day, thoughts of what might have been filled Thomas's brain. When he was ripped from Kawai's arms, those emotions never left.

Part of Thomas knew that he couldn't have changed the sequence of events with Kawai. There's no scenario where he never leaves her side, or they live a perfect, love-filled life together without him going to the Pacific. With Lance, there was no reassurance of reality. The reality of the situation was that Thomas could have saved his best friend, squad leader, and right-hand man.

If he reacted earlier, saw his plane sooner, or suggested a different strategy during intelligence meetings— maybe sleeping instead of worrying about Kawai on nights before training. Building bonds with the men, without cutting it short, to write the 'ghost' on his mind. Walking out of the Christmas dinner and not reacting to Lance's tirade about Kawai and putting his ego aside to admit faults or even follow Lance from the beginning of the battle, instead of taking on two fighters alone. If he did all those things or even just a few, maybe Lance would be sitting beside him, celebrating Christmas with a cold brew and busting on Thomas for watching a pointless bird.

The New Year, 1944, bloomed like the most hideous of flowers. Spring came with a dangerous storm of bullets, bombs, and intelligence reports. Summer heat brought frustration and desperation. Could they be home by next Christmas? Possibly, but every year seemed to bring only that false sense of hope. A feeling which seemed fabricated to make the men believe and push through the lonely, hot nights and endless missions. For Thomas, each sunrise without Lance seemed to be nearly the same through the sunset before the first anniversary.

With each training exercise, patrol and escort, Thomas battled with his thoughts. The war had become a backdrop to a much larger battle within. Hundreds of hours of thinking, debating, and misleading. Convincing himself that he was the reason Lance was gone one minute, just to let enough logic in the next. Whenever time allowed, he was parked like a cement block in Lance's favorite chair, accompanied by the unopened six-pack and blank pieces of paper.

Thomas's ability to write Kawai was gone. There were no more words left to say. Hundreds of 'I love you's' went unanswered. Dreams left without reassurance and pain at every signature meant Thomas had nothing left to give. When Thomas learned of his letters not being sent, he decided to keep writing them, hoping to document his everyday experiences and share them with Kawai when he returned to O'ahu. Now, too much regret and embarrassment filled his mind to write a single word of what each day was like for him.

As the bird flew from pole to pole, attempts at drawing Hope were all Thomas could muster whenever it visited the destroyer. He couldn't understand why the bird kept coming back, but he was sure it was because of the sailors above him feeding it now and then. Whatever the reason, it was the only positivity and source of happiness Thomas could draw from.

The Pacific Plover made Thomas wonder if Kawai had passed away, and this was her way of visiting him. Those morbid thoughts always led to grabbing one of the six sealed brews. Thomas pondered what kind of drunk he would be as his finger flipped the slightly opened metal tab that protected him from a complete loss of self-control. Front and back, he messed with the tab, thinking of his father.

A shot to honor Lance and the others lost a year earlier commenced without Thomas's participation. He had made his way to the same spot he thought away the 365-days before. Today would be no different. The wind blew sternly as the bird that had kept his mind somewhat at ease, and a small glimmer of hope in his heart, was nowhere to be found.

Maybe Hope could feel the tension of the day and made the right decision to stay away? Whatever the reason, it played a part in Thomas hitting rock bottom with his thoughts. No evening could top this one. Not the first night after Pearl and losing Kawai, the disappointment of not returning home to her letter after his maiden mission, or even Lance dying. There was no end to the war in sight, no matter how much everyone talked about it. Tomorrow wouldn't bring Kawai back, lessen the pain of seeing Lance's plane hit the water or change the depression that filled Thomas's mind.

As he looked over the water crashing against the carrier, Thomas wondered how many men reached their final resting spot below. How much pain, regret, or helplessness did they feel when the end was inevitable? Did those soldiers, fighting for the same reasons Lance did write home? Were their folks aware of how they felt about them and how much love was in their heart?

With doubt and hopelessness at an all-time high, Thomas reached for the six-pack that he brought. He replaced it with a fresh, never opened one each time the previous beer expired. Like everything else in his life, his actions when grabbing a warm one were the same; flipping the tab, thinking about the direction his life had gone and what his deadbeat father would do in the same situation, never daring to open the can.

This time was different. Every ounce of self-control and care of defeating the pain naturally had left. Thomas placed his right hand over the can, clinching his fingers under the tab and pulling up. A tear fell down his face, and a lump entered his throat as the sound that most viewed as refreshing made Thomas's mind race even faster. Abusing the liquid just a few inches from his lips cost his father a marriage to his high school sweetheart, a booming business that Thomas's grandparents had built, and a relationship with his son. The beautiful life the Metic family had and the peaceful childhood Thomas had grown accustomed to was drowned in the carelessness of one man. A man he couldn't speak the name of and hadn't for years put the bottle above his own family—proof above providing and numbness over love.

That was irrelevant to Thomas as he stared at the can, and the swishing liquid inside, as a sunset that he would appreciate every second of in a previous life, lit up the horizon. His father had ruined a life that took years to build by putting the bottle above his family. Thomas understood that, even in this moment of helplessness, but that was what drew him to take a sip and let himself go. Beer and eventually liquor made his dad's wife unfaithful, their bank account dry up, and relationship with his son go to hell, but Thomas didn't have any of that.

The woman he loved was hours away, if alive at all; his career had given him a dead friend and a mind full of doubt, not to mention that even the thought of kids made him even angrier. If it wasn't the twins Kawai dreamed of and lit up talking about, Thomas didn't want any, and besides, who was he to raise any children? He couldn't even protect the men he was assigned to. A life full of pain and disappointment had led to this moment. It was time to finally find anything to put a damper on the agony inside.

"That one for me?" An approaching voice asked as a startled Thomas turned towards Commander Styles, spilling a bit of the beer on himself. "Uh, yes, sir, have at it. I can't have it anyway."

"Why can't yah?" Commander Styles asked as he tipped the beer back, throwing a chair beside Thomas. "A cold one after a long day never hurt anyone."

"My dad was a stubborn drunk," Thomas said, turning his head towards Styles, with his aviators protecting his watering eyes. "Just can't risk it."

"Well, you sure risk the stubborn part," Commander Styles said sternly as he put his feet on the railing."

"Sir?" Thomas asked respectfully.

"Don't sir me, Metic," Styles said, frustrated. "You come out here every damn night; whenever I walk by, you're always here with a pack of unopened beer and an empty notepad. The pad is still empty when you leave, and none of these are opened. I know what you're doing. You're blaming yourself for everything that has gone on over the past few years in your life. You leaving that girl? Nothing you could do. Lance dying? You're the exact reason he had a fighting chance; that mission made you an Ace, for God's sake!"

"I feel like I could have done more," Thomas said, trying not to let the emotion he felt come out.

"No, you wish you could have done more; there's a difference," Styles said, smashing the newly emptied can with his foot and reaching for another. "I don't blame you for not drinking these, that's your choice and an admirable one, but you're slowly killing yourself in other, more harmful ways. We all wish we could do more. All of you are under my command, and though I'm supposed to keep my distance to lead you without emotion, you're all like sons to me. It hurts me more than you know when one of you doesn't come back. I miss my wife more than anything, and yes, it's far different than your situation, but we are all away from our loved ones. Letters take days, maybe weeks, to reach home. By the time they do, everything could change. You may be better off not knowing."

"Her well-being scares me," Thomas said, fiddling with the paper in his lap. "If I at least knew she was alive and didn't die that day, I wouldn't worry as much."

"You wouldn't?" Commander Styles asked sarcastically. "That's bullshit. You'd worry more because you're a helluva man. You'd push harder to get home faster and hang your emotions on every letter. You don't know, I get that, but focus on the things you do know. You've made it through situations that most pilots haven't. If there's anyone who should appreciate that, it's you. Any man who makes it through this war alive, with all four of his limbs and a functional state of mind, is destined for far greater things. Find God and pray for that. Pray for the chance to return home and ask for the strength to get through the things you don't believe you can. He's there, and I may not be a religious man, but if I return home to my wife and kids, the man upstairs had something to do with it. The same goes for you."

"Yeah," Thomas uttered, struggling to find the right words. "Hope I get to see her again, is all."

"Lt. Jones had a harsh way of explaining his position, but he had a solid one," Styles said in-between drinks. "Chasing ghosts, people, unfortunate events you couldn't control, and outcomes you have no business trying to manifest does nothing. That's all he was trying to say at that Christmas party, not in a good way, but from a solid place. Forget the others for a minute; if you sit and wallow in the negativity from the past or unknown of the future, you'll die without recognizing the present or ever experiencing that very future you're obsessing about. Let it go. Don't let her go; let the regret, doubt, and worry fade. Replace that with the good memories, the love that we both know is still there, and believe that you're still here for a reason. That reason may include her, it may not, but wouldn't it be nice to find out?"

"There's nothing more in this world I want than to find that out," Thomas said with a smirk and sniffle.

"It's hard; all of this is. *Life* is," Commander Styles said as he stood and placed his hand on Thomas's shoulder. "There is some good news, though. Relations with locals in Hawaii are improving, and your letters may get to be sent soon, after all. Look forward to that, but don't dwell on it and if you want to honor Lance, lead these men in the sky better than ever. Be the best pilot you can be when you close that canopy and know that he had a fighting chance because of you. The rest of the men deserve that same chance. Some big things are coming up soon; we need our best pilots and leaders at full potential."

Commander Styles had a unique way of breaking his men down, then building them up higher than they ever thought possible, all within a conversation. His words cut deep but opened one's eyes to the positive side of reality. Thomas realized that he had a history of overstating things. When it came to the war ending, Styles beat the "we'll be home by Christmas" drum the loudest. He'd put that hopeful, almost desperate statement into the ether every year around this time. Relations with locals may be improving, but Thomas had come to grips long ago that he'd never receive a letter from Kawai. It would be a fairytale, face-to-face conversation if he heard from her again.

Everything Styles had to say, though exaggerated at every word, made painful sense. Thomas knew he had to put it all on pause. Forget the negativity, numb the pain with prayer and focus on the present. Lance would want him to move on and stop chasing the regretful reality of that day. Nothing Thomas could do now would bring Lance back. He knew he'd never fully get over the pain or think he did everything in his power to save his best friend; there were dozens of other men who would have desperation in their eyes, looking to Lt. Metic to lead them when the next mission came.

There wasn't a battle Thomas could win, move he could make, or plane he could shoot down that would bring Lance back. No letter he wrote, tear he cried, or dream he dreamt would put Kawai back in his arms, with sand under their feet. That was his reality, a painful reality, but one he had to find a way to deal with.

The next battle won, positive move made, and Japanese plane that hit the ocean floor may not bring his right-hand man back, but it would bring each of the other men that much closer to returning to their families. Successful and safe missions were the only way Thomas would ever walk up to the door of the Jones household and tell them stories of their heroic son. Winning the war would be the only path to discovering Kawai's well-being and experiencing all of the family events Lance would never get the chance to. Wedding bells, baby strollers, and golden years on the porch with Kawai required a win in the Pacific, one that an overly enthused Commander Styles made Thomas believe was close.

Ever since the moment Kawai and Thomas's lives went in sudden miss-direction, the Navy had challenged Thomas. Though this was unfair, in his mind at times, he wasn't alone. Every man around him, as Styles noted, was fighting their own hardships. The truth was, the Navy had forged Thomas a life away from the dead-end path of his family's farm, showed him what true love was, and gave him a best friend to honor. Whether on the surface of his heavy mind or deep below his thoughts, Thomas always knew the battles in front of him were worth fighting, some moments were simply easier to notice than others and varied with every event. Everything had come full circle, Lance, Kawai, his grandparents, and the men around him; Thomas was fighting for each of them, all along.

From the time we're born, each person has their hourglass. Timelines filled with sand, some with more than others. That's God's novel. A beautiful script written in the clouds, never to be seen by the naked eye. No matter the regret or pain, there was nothing Thomas could do to reverse that. Lance's sand ran out, fighting for his country across the Pacific. There was none to be added, nothing to be erased or re-written. Kawai's story could also be written with a short chapter titled "48-Hours with Thomas," or it could be paused, waiting for Lt. Metic to return and continue writing a beautiful fairytale. It was out of Thomas's control and into the hands of a God he was re-introducing himself to.

Thomas didn't become a religious man overnight, but the July conversation with Commander Styles played over in his mind as the summer days passed slowly and autumn set in. Praying became more frequent, committed to talking to God through everyday scenarios and each night before he laid his head down to rest, instead of only in dire situations or before missions. When the war first began and Kawai was taken from him, Thomas asked God to protect him, bring her back, or hurry the adverse events along so that he could return safely to her. Praying helped ease his mind during those stressful moments, but only briefly, until the adrenaline took over or something distracted him from the pain.

With critical, outcome-altering events on the horizon, as Commander Styles made known, Thomas felt added pressure to find something to ease the pain he felt, permanently, or at least to the point he didn't have to concentrate on it any longer. Drinking wasn't an option; no matter how much he tried to convince himself that he wasn't his father, even the most persuasive people couldn't convince him to tip one back. Like the rest of the pilots, writing to his loved ones would only bring more overthinking and painful realities to the forefront, leading to sleepless nights that would be detrimental to his performance in the air.

Talking to God and putting a micro-focus into the task at hand was all Thomas could do to pass the time outside of his plane. No magic words or actions could be taken to make the time go faster until he saw Kawai or learned of her condition. Nothing he did would bring his best friend back or change the thoughts that bounced around in his head but praying may just give him the strength to conquer all and at the very least touch down on the O'ahu runway in one piece.

Thomas remembered going to church on special occasions as a child. Easter and Christmas Eve stood out as times that the family would get dressed up, attend mass, and then enjoy a meal together with other church members. His parents were too busy or disconnected with their faith to care about taking him every Sunday, so once his grandma and grandpa passed away, those special trips to church went with them.

His grandparents were very religious, giving their life and being to their faith. If something happened positively to either of them, it was a blessing from the heavens above, and all adverse events happened for a reason, even if it wasn't apparent to the naked eye what that reason was. 'God didn't give anyone more than they could handle,' his grandma would say, and though Thomas respected his grandparents more than anyone else, he wasn't sure what to think about that. Life had given him more curveballs in only a few decades than most experience in a lifetime. The war and missing Kawai made him question even the most fundamental aspects of his faith, but when the going got tough, Thomas always hit his knees, begging God or whoever else was listening to see him through.

"The Lord isn't a wishing well," his grandfather would recite. "All you can do is live your life to the best of your ability, control what you can control, and ask for strength to weather the rest."

There was no time before when Thomas needed more strength than he did right now. At any time, he could be called on to lead a group of nervous and anxious men into battles. Whether it was Lance or other pilots that had perished, very few experienced airmen remained. Thomas was the only pilot in his squadron that had been on every mission assigned to them; everyone else had either perished or been transferred to fight in Europe. The pressure was at an all-time high, and prayer was the only tool Thomas was equipped to deal with it.

Leading his men, getting them home to their families, returning to find out if the future would include the woman he loved, and honoring his wingman's life outside of the war, was the objective and the strength he received from God was how he would accomplish it. Prayer was powerful and trying to find a relationship with his faith was helping, as the last day of August 1944 was crossed out in red on the calendar beside Thomas's bed, but it wasn't an end-all.

Missing Kawai never left his heart, and nights by the water didn't leave Thomas's routine. Instead of being joined by an unopened six-pack and a blank notepad, he was alone, with his thoughts and an occasional visit from Hope. Commander Styles had left a mark on Thomas when they spoke on the anniversary of Lance's death. Not only had he found the ear of his lord again, but the only reminiscing and thinking he did was recounting the good times that made his heart feel whole instead of broken.

Pranks and the laughter Lance brought into his life when the two were paired together as roommates at Pearl made him feel closer to his lost friend. Lance did just a few things to irritate and anger his uptight roommate by changing the time on Thomas's alarm clock, hiding his boots, and putting wrinkles in his undershirts. It was because of Lance and his playful arrogance that brought Kawai into Thomas's life. Thomas would have never met her if it wasn't for the constant pandering to get him to go out.

Recalling that evening always made him laugh. Thomas agreed to go to the theater to tell Lance he didn't have fun, never hear about it again or return to base, to rejoin his strict schedule and job he was so focused on. Seeing Kawai and her unforgettably beautiful smile erased Lance from his mind at that moment, staring across the theater floor. Remembering it now did the same, as he sat on the deck, with nothing but the sound of waves and the carrier cutting through the water, playing in the background.

Before the war, every minute spent with Kawai or memory of the first time he saw her made every thought of negativity from his past or fear of the future leave. She was all that mattered, a symbol of hope and the beauty that still existed. His dad's alcoholism, his mom's unfaithfulness, and the deaths of his grandparents were filed into the back of his mind. Worries of a possible war and headlines of the advancements made by Hitler or the Japanese were put on pause. The only thing that mattered was sitting in those memories or savoring every second with the most gorgeous woman God ever created.

Years after that memorable moment and the nights they spent together, Kawai still made Thomas forget about everything else on his mind when he thought of her, but in a far different manner. She no longer brought only positive thoughts or hope for tomorrow. The same feelings of sadness he fought with when remembering his parents, grandparents, or the night he lost Lance now were associated with the woman he still loved so dearly.

When the sadness became too unbearable, Thomas reminded himself of Commander Styles's words of wisdom; to control the controllable, leave the uncontrollable to God, and find a memory that would bring him a sense of hope. Thomas had covered almost every second he could muster, looking back on the short time he had spent with Kawai. He struggled with recalling moments he hadn't in a while or snippets that would relieve his mind of the pain and let it focus on the love his heart wanted so bad to be noticed.

With the sun beneath the horizon and an all-too-familiar scene of darkness set the stage on all sides of Thomas and his chair, an odd sense of peace fell over him as he investigated a sky full of stars. When his mind would generally be racing, all he felt was peace.

"All those beautiful stars," Kawai said as her memory began to return to Thomas. "I have never gotten used to them; they still amaze me and humble my mind."

"Growing up, I never took the time to notice them," Thomas uttered. "This may be the first night I have actually laid down and just stared into the sky."

"When the first Hawaiians came to the islands, they were led by them," Kawai said softly with a smile almost as bright. "The wind and the stars led them to create our culture, which is why I'm here."

"They led you to me," Thomas said as he held her just a bit tighter, kissing the side of her head.

"This war will take you away from me," Kawai said quietly, never taking her eyes off the illuminated sky.

"Don't talk like that," Thomas replied in disbelief.

"It's okay," she responded, reaching her hand up to grace his neck. "They'll do exactly what they've always done. The stars will lead you through every battle, mission, and whatever else stands in your way. You'll find your way back into my arms; just follow the stars."

The memory of her voice and the confidence she had in every word turned into a dream as Thomas faded to sleep beneath those same stars, thousands of miles away from the sandy beaches of O'ahu. Every prayer he said, time he put his trust into God, and the moment he felt empty, the man upstairs led him back to the woman he loved. Nights of struggling to remember the good times they shared were gone, and memories he hadn't thought of in years, resurfaced. Each time he knelt beside his bed or fell to his knees against the railing, desperate for strength to get through the day, peace followed.

God, Lance pushing him through, Kawai looking down on him or the necklace that bared her initials, her future daughter and the women that came before her, whatever it was, his mind always went peaceful. Each time he prayed, begging for strength and pleading for an avenue to a positive future, he was given it. Just enough to ease himself and the courage to force himself to focus on a memory that brought him happiness instead of the overwhelming sense of sadness he had drawn so accustomed to.

"Metic, Metic," Commander Styles yelled, waking Thomas as he ran up to his chair.

Thomas scrambled to his feet, following Styles into a room, where dozens of tired men awaited the news of what was going on. Even though Thomas had been through this very feeling of unknown a few times, the inexperience of the pilots around him made the severity of the moment much stronger.

"Gentlemen, we have reached a critical moment in our affairs against the Japanese," Commander Styles began. "Each mission is more important than the one before. Every battle, bomb dropped, and yard gained could mean a week shaved off the time before we're all home."

"Home" had become the most powerful four-letter word in the United States Navy, as some pilots, like Thomas, hadn't seen their loved ones in a few years. The very mention of returning home or the chance of that day coming sooner than expected sent shock waves through the dimly lit room. Men that were still feeling the effects of a night of drinking felt sober as a teen in Sunday school. Fatigue from being awoken in the dead of night didn't matter anymore. Every man sat up straight, wiped the sleep from their eyes, and hung on every word Commander Styles uttered.

"Every one of you will be placed into Task Forces, which will strike various Japanese Installations at Formosa," Commander Styles said with a stern look, as some of the men looked at each other with excited grins and clapped. "We're going to take out as much of their airpower as possible, opening up the opportunity for future missions. The mission will launch Thursday morning, under cover of darkness and will be multiple waves over a few days."

In the matter of a few minutes, Thomas had gone from dreaming of Kawai and a memory that made him feel closer to her than he had in months to orders for a mission that could bring her back into his arms sooner than expected. If this battle went through as planned, with minimal loss and substantial ground gained, just maybe he could be on a plane back to O'ahu by Christmas and know if the woman he loved was still waiting on him.

Launching for a mission had changed very little since the first one Thomas participated in, but there were a few noticeable differences this time. Lance wasn't in the briefings, making jokes about the intelligence that was mostly always wrong or bringing a much-needed comedic relief to the anxious moment leading up to cranking the engines. Kawai was on Thomas's mind, but with a calm mind as he stared at the stars that filled the early morning sky. Dawn was nearing, but he could see them as clearly as the night

Kawai brushed his face while ensuring that they would bring him back to her.

Emotions of the first moment Thomas became one with the plane and the canopy closed was one aspect that changed with each mission he took part in. Excitement raced through his mind as the final moments wore off before cranking the propellers during his maiden voyage in the Pacific; he couldn't wait to return and opened the letter he thought was from Kawai. The last mission he took part in, an opposite feeling of panic and worry for his best friend, leading the Squadron for the first time, and doubt about his ability to make decisions filled the mind of Thomas.

This time, he was at peace with it all. At ease with the task at hand, losing his best friend and missing the woman he still hoped would become his wife. Prayer, the confidence and perspective given from Commander Styles a few months prior, or the positive memories of Kawai that now filled his headspace during every event that brought unknowns all provided the perfect combination for a battered pilot.

Thomas's pre-launch prayer was similar each time he recited it but was only dominated by requests for strength this time. Strength to lead his men, return them to their families and let them overcome any inexperience that may hinder their progress. He asked God to guide him, take the wings of his plane, and put them alongside the plan He had for Thomas's life.

Kawai's necklace sat between his hands during every pre-launch prayer. Thomas no longer cared about the necklace losing her scent, however, as he relied on God and destiny to keep her memory alive. It was the only object Thomas had to remind himself of her, and that was to be cherished, not saved for special occasions. He sometimes wore the necklace to bed when he felt lonely or on a patrol that he wasn't feeling strong enough for. On missions like the one he was getting ready for, he would place the necklace around his wrist, tightly under the shirt and equipment that rubbed against his skin.

Once in the air, there was a job to do, men to lead, and a country to defend. Unlike previous missions, Lance, Kawai, nor his grandparents, were on his mind. It was all business this time around. Whether because of his newfound faith, the pressure of leading pilots into battle, or his previous experience, Thomas was calm and ready to do his job.

The squadron was anxious for the first wave but confident that they would come away with little to no loss, as the darkness of early morning dawn and the element of surprise would give them the edge on day one. Many of the pilots were taking part in their first combat mission of this magnitude. Thomas knew they were nervous, he was too, but he had to be solid. A leader that wouldn't break or let his mind scramble when the task at hand required the highest level of focus.

Water crashing against the sand as the Squadron reached small islands between themselves and their target presented Thomas with a crossroads. He could let the beach take his mind to memories of Kawai, use that as his motivation and perform at a high level. That mindset had helped him before, but it was selfish and against everything Commander Styles expected from him. The battle may be won, and

Thomas could become even more of an Ace, but the Squadron could also lose many pilots due to their inexperience and the lack of leadership around them. This time, on this mission, Kawai, honoring Lance and trying to prove his parents wrong, had to come second. At this moment, he had to become a leader who put his men before himself, even if it meant the ultimate price.

A decision was made in the mind of Thomas Metic, looking over open seas preparing for the coastline; lay it all on the line for his men and their families, not his own. Thomas knew if he were meant to come out of the mission alive, God would make that happen, one way or another, but regardless of the man's faith to the left or right of him, he was their protection and strength.

The October sunset painted an ominous, nervous scene as Thomas prepared to key his mic and break radio silence. Everything Thomas had done led him to this moment. For his entire Naval career, Thomas was all about himself. Whether to push his career further, use it as an outlet to prove his family wrong, or help forget the pain of the present, he had never been the leader he vowed to be. On this first of multiple potential stressful days, he could right all the wrongs and miss-steps of his time in the air with a flawless mission. Bringing absolutely no loss home was the goal. Many would argue that was an unrealistic ambition, but as a man who had not even lived to see his 30th birthday kissed his worn glove protected right index and middle finger, to kiss the initials of a woman he may never see again, those goals filled his mind. Thomas's hand shook as he put it back on the yoke, preparing to speak, but his mind remained focused and calm. They were only miles from the target.

"Alright, gentlemen, it shouldn't be too much longer—" Thomas began saying as the squadron was flanked on all sides.

The feeling that ripped through Thomas's mind was all too familiar. From being in control to having a one-way ticket to death placed at his doorstep, with zero time to pack. If he was going to be remembered as a good leader, someone who protected his men at all costs and returned them home in significant numbers, Thomas had to deal with a few things quickly. This wasn't the battle that Lance died in. Nothing he would do over the next few minutes would bring his friend back or avenge his death. Commander Styles nor anyone in the Squadron blamed Thomas for Lt. Jones's death, and they trusted him to lead them into battle and the hell that was commencing all around them.

'Trust God, trust God, trust God,' played like clockwork in Thomas's head as he sprang into action. An inexperienced pilot, one of the men Thomas was extra focused on protecting, was already trailing smoke, with multiple Japanese fighters close behind. Without hesitation or looking back on the similar sequence of events that took his friend's life, Thomas dropped altitude and jumped in behind the fighters painting his brother's wing with bullets.

Thomas pegged his throttle wide open. His plane flew at its full potential, with his right index and middle fingers ready for the perfect time to strike. *'Not yet, not yet, not yet, now!'* Thomas said softly to himself. With a few thrusts of the trigger, there was one less plane between the safety of one of his men and their death. There was zero time for celebration, as Thomas didn't react even the slightest to yet another confirmed kill. Statistics meant nothing if there was another tally in the United States Killed in Action column.

Today wouldn't be the day another American Pilot died on the watch of Lt. Metic. He may not be able to avenge the past, but he could shape the future of the man's life he was now assigned to protect in a positive light. With every bit of courage and strength he could muster, down went another Japanese fighter, and the smoke trailed the American plane carrying a man with a family of his own was safe.

Thomas circled around and scanned the smoke-filled sky for other pilots to assist; the job was far from finished. The only problem was that he had no one doing the same for him. The Japanese swarmed Thomas's Hellcat from both sides before he could react, one from the west and another from directly above his canopy. Rounds pierced the F6F's right-wing and engine compartment. There were multiple irreversible failures.

Thomas had extraordinarily little time to think or come to grips with what was happening. There was no time to dwell or reminisce on his life as the engine shut off, forcing the plane into a full descent over enemy-riddled territory. A man who had put everything on the line to protect his men had to bail. One who had lost a friend in a far too similar sequence didn't know if the woman he loved was alive or dead and had no family to miss, faced the possibility of his own mortality.

With the canopy forced open, Thomas jumped into a free-fall, with only the strength he had prayed for at his back, pulling his parachute and instantly searching for the pistol that would bring his only protection. The gun was nowhere to be found. Zero protection from Japanese sailors and patrols. Nothing to keep them from shooting his defenseless body out of the air, a body that had not been physically harmed yet, but had taken the biggest of its mental hits to date. Thomas's mind went numb. He knew there wasn't anything to protect him. There were no carriers nearby to rescue him and zero U.S. patrols on the small islands that lined his view.

This entire mission, Thomas had forced himself to think about helping his men, protecting their interests, and returning them home to their loved ones, and he was proud of that. At this moment, however, while he dangled from a few loose strings with just feet between him and a bath with hell, all he saw was her face. In the clouds, water below him, and sky that painted the scenery to his horror story was Kawai. As he hit the water with a splash that could be noticeable from miles away, his mind returned to peace.

She was with him. Whether in spirit, upstairs with the lord, Lance, and his grandparents, or in a symbolic way, through the necklace she gave him, that was still wrapped around his wrist, somehow surviving the fall. In separating himself from the 'shute, Thomas floated on his back, eyes closed, letting the waves and the destiny God had planned for him lead his body, as his mind focused on the woman who found a way to calm him, even in the darkest of moments.

"Do you know how to float?" Kawai asked with a deep breath after racing Thomas to the ocean.

"No, not a clue," Thomas said with a shy laugh.

"Watch me," she said as she laid down in the shallow, calm water. "You just spread your arms, balance your back and move your legs with the waves."

"Easier said than done," Thomas said as he tried to mimic her movements.

"You're trying too hard," Kawai said, holding back a laugh. "Close your eyes."

"How does that help?" Thomas mumbled as he grew frustrated with falling back first into the water.

"You have to trust," Kawai uttered softly, placing her hands under Thomas's back. "Close your eyes and trust that the water will hold you. The water has helped give life to millions of Hawaiians; it can hold you if you just trust. Let the ocean move you. It will take you where you need to be."

"Like this?" Thomas asked, opening one eye.

"Just like that," Kawai said with a laugh, reaching down to kiss Thomas's floating body.

"I trust you," Thomas said, as his mind harshly came to the grim reality placed in front of him.

"Welcome to the beginning of the end," a man said in broken English as Thomas opened his eyes on the beach, with water crashing against his body, seeing four Japanese patrols with guns drawn.

CHAPTER 9

The floor was wet and cold. The room as dark as the souls that attacked Thomas's nation, ripped his woman away from him, and dragged him into what they hoped would be his final resting place. Clothes torn, with mud and dirt caked against every inch of his wounded body. Beaten to a breaking point, he refused to react and had little movement for the energy he struggled to muster. Thomas Metic was a Prisoner of War and sentenced to a life of slaving for Satan.

There was very little memory of how he had gotten to this window-less room. Thomas had no idea through the beatings, scrambled mind, and hood placed over his head when transported. All he knew was he was alone, cold, and hurt; injured mentally and physically. He couldn't believe that a life that showed so much promise during the early days of December 1941 had turned so horrific in the Autumn of 1944. There was no telling how much time had passed or how long Thomas had been out. Did he fall unconscious? How bad were his wounds? Would he even be able to walk when demanded?

Thomas faced what felt like a wall made out of dirt and poorly placed stone. He struggled to turn his body and could hardly raise his arms to twist himself or lock his fingers to say a prayer. The ground grew colder by the second as his left arm became numb, supporting the weight of his weary body. Thomas's battered legs felt like thousand-pound boulders as he touched his abused ribs, examining what he was sure was a break, or two, in them.

He was unable to move and scared to make too much noise, fearing what could come next if a Japanese guard had heard him. Thomas remembered horrific rumors spread through the squadron about how American troops were treated when captured. There was nothing positive about it, and every man that gave their opinion on the subject would rather be dead than placed in a POW camp, slaving by day and starving by night.

Thomas wondered how he had gotten to that point as he stared into the pitch-black room leading to nowhere. The space was so dark he couldn't tell how big it was; for all he knew, there was a man on the other side of the room in the same position or somewhere as small as his grandparent's outhouse. Nothing kept his mind from racing, and right now, he couldn't muster the strength to say a prayer. Everything that Thomas had been through had led to this, but why?

When he joined the Navy, it seemed so promising. As a dripping sound and faint conversations in Japanese laid background music to a nightmare, Thomas tried to come to grips with his ever-changing reality. He remembered how happy and purposeful he felt when he flew by himself for the first time. Even stronger feelings of pride came with every new responsibility, challenge, and change that led him through his career. Of course, those new experiences brought something positive until December 7th, 1941.

"The date which will live in infamy," as President Franklin said so eloquently, had affected millions of Americans negatively. Still, Thomas couldn't understand why his life had taken such a

drastic turn. Not only did he lose his best friend in combat, which wasn't a special story, given how many other soldiers had the same reality, but with no family left to write home about and the woman he loved possibly already gone, Thomas struggled to find purpose. There was no clear answer to why he was there or the choices that sent his life spinning out of control. If Thomas didn't join the military when he did, the government would have drafted him anyway, and he would have never met Kawai, so there was no sense in dwelling over that what if, either.

Thomas had gotten used to facing new obstacles, he had dealt with many over the past three years, but this one took the cake. Even with all of the negativity and challenges thrown his way, he found God, a purpose in the war, and trusted Commander Styles' word, all after being physically ripped from the arms of his other half and losing his better half in the skies. He did everything that was asked of him and more, just to be the mule of a country that wished him dead.

Doubt in every aspect of his life set in. Facing the reality that this could be where he took his last breath and never having the chance to find Kawai again was unbearable. No turning at their wedding to see the most gorgeous bride walking towards him and lifting her veil to lay those piercing brown eyes on him, with the most innocent of perfect smiles. Children playing in the yard or grandkids listening to stories on the porch, like Thomas did when he was little, were becoming less and less likely of possible events in his future. Thomas did his best to close his eyes and imagine a positive future, something he had done since his conversation with Commander Styles on the deck.

Kawai would be there, beautiful from her early-30s to her golden years. Kids, grandkids, great-grandkids, a huge family, and laughter with every manifested event. They would own the winery and the theater, taking advantage of a booming, peaceful American economy. Thomas would visit Lance's family every few holidays, telling them stories of his heroism and the jokes he'd play. A simple man with what he thought were simple dreams. The woman he loved by his side and kids to share their love with. He didn't need to strike a million, own fancy things, or celebrate a birthday with three-numbered candles. All he wanted, needed, and prayed for started with one woman and grew with her, but that dream seemed less and less likely with every event he faced in the Pacific.

Tears began to fall as the reality of Thomas's situation settled in his mind. He tried once more to forcefully flip himself over, looking for any sense of physical comfort he could find. Strength wasn't a strong suit for him, and as he repeatedly tried on the damp earthly floor, using his right hand to pull his body weight over to that side, he slipped. Instead of gently rolling his body to his right side, Thomas's hand slipped, and he smashed into the ground.

Whether mental pain or physical, Thomas's emotions grew stronger, and before he knew it, he was crying harder than ever. Tears poured, and sobs of built-up pain followed. There was no being quiet now. Thomas knew that no pain from any guard could match what he was feeling inside. Hopeless moments were a theme of the war, but he had found ways to finally cope with them and then, this. The hurt he was experiencing at this moment was deeper than losing the grip on

Kawai's hand that fateful day or knowing she'd never be able to send him a letter.

Each hopeless night was filled with agony, and the belief that he would ever see her face again lessened with every unfortunate occurrence. Still, he'd always find a memory, thought, or a bit of strength to convince himself he would see her again. Thomas's anger continued to build as he fully persuaded himself that he would never make it out of this room, let alone know the woman he loved again. This frustration was followed by smacking his hand, over-and-over on the floor beside him. The injuries to his body hampered his ability to punch the wall or find a guard for fighting as he wanted, so he settled for a toddler-like show of aggression.

Thomas was ready to give up, wait for himself to be beaten to death or starved. His will to fight was gone, and all that came to his mind was finding something to ease the pain. There was no watching the waves crash or writing a letter for therapy. No conversations with Commander Styles, and his faith had been challenged so much he refused to speak to God. All was said in done in Thomas's mind until fate stepped in, once more.

As he slapped his hand repeatedly on what felt like damp dirt, he noticed an object; Thomas first thought it was some type of wire or foreign animal, which frightened him until he felt something that, just like many moments during his time in the Pacific, changed his mindset. Kawai's necklace was right there beside him, or what was left of it anyway. A quick examination led to Thomas realizing that another man or an impact he had taken along the way had broken the necklace up bad. The Brown Pearl that reminded him each time of her flawless eyes was gone, as well as most of the beads that barred the initials of Kawai, important women from her family and a spot for her future first-born daughter.

As Thomas attempted to feel along the string, he found two beads left behind, which seemed to be in perfect shape. With most of the feeling in his hands gone due to the extreme pain he felt, there was no telling whose initials they represented, but that didn't matter. It was a miracle the necklace had survived what Thomas had been through. A fall from hundreds of feet in the air, a crash into the water, countless beatings from guards, and only God-knows-what else, yet it was still there, right with him like it had been since the day Kawai gave the necklace to him. Some of it was gone, all of it was battered, but Thomas viewed that as a symbol for where he was in his life.

Eyes closed and body at a sleepy, numb ease, Thomas wondered what God was trying to tell him. God had let him go through so many downs yet gave him enough belief to keep pushing each time. Whether the letter that wasn't meant to be, sending Commander Styles to talk some sense into him, or now, the necklace that had been through hell and back with him, Thomas knew his lord above was telling him to just hang in there and believe. Like the necklace and two beads left, Thomas was on his last leg, with not much to pull through with and a shell of his former self, but he was still there.

Symbols are a way of life in Hawaiian culture, and whether Kawai knew her necklace would bring Thomas so much strength or not, it had. The torn string and faceless beads had calmed his mind, once again, in the deepest of hell, with Satan just feet away. Thomas didn't know if it was Kawai's spirit riding through this roller coaster, with mostly downhill tracks, or the direction of the women before her, leading Thomas back to the love of his life. Whatever the force, it was strong, and Thomas wasn't going to be allowed just to give up.

The chance of seeing Kawai again was low, and Thomas knew that, but it wasn't impossible. Thomas decided at that moment, with the faint sounds of hell just behind the unrecognizable door, that he would once again fight on. This time, the fight would be different. Completely mental, with no weapons at his disposal, his war was between the ears now. A place he had gotten lost many times since leaving O'ahu, he would have to find the strength and courage to win now.

Drips of water played the melody to a song that Thomas wasn't sure the lyrics to or what the next note may bring. His body was aching. Every bone felt bruised or broken, with each movement bringing a grimace and sharp breath. Thomas's mind remained at peace but very tired as he held the fragile necklace in his sore palm. There was no set schedule to the working day of a prisoner of war, and the stories Thomas had heard were all but fair. He knew that any chance given to catch some shut eye and rest, no matter the circumstances or possibilities of tomorrow behind the infamous door that had yet to be seen, had to be taken.

Hiding the necklace somewhere safe was the last order of business before Thomas rested his eyes. The

Japanese guards had done their damnedest to destroy it once already, just like they would try to do to Thomas, every day until he either died or was rescued, but in his mind, like with the strong beads, they would fail. After a few minutes of rubbing his hands up and down the walls and floor beneath him, looking for anything to pile together on the necklace or a spot to shove it into, Thomas found a crevasse in the wall.

It was unclear how much protection the spot he found would lend to the necklace, but he had to try. With no light around him to see, he was taking a chance, as any sign to the Japanese that he was hiding something from them would mean trouble for what was left of his well-being. Thomas did his best to arrange it to where he couldn't feel the string of beads from where he sat, hoping that meant they weren't obvious to the naked eye. Lasting several minutes, it was a task Thomas had to get right. Pushing it as far into the small hole as the string would go, placing loose dirt around him into the crevasse, and feeling it under his hand wouldn't move any longer from exhaustion was all his body allowed. How the necklace was would have to be okay, as he slumped onto his side, unable to move another inch. Thomas's body was tired, and his mind was at peace. Calmness from the heavens above or spirits around made Thomas drift into a fast sleep and dream, about a blessing he could only wish to receive.

The love of his life, in the most gorgeous white pa'u, magenta bustier top, and white lei around her neck, flashed through a dancing, damaged mind. Kawai was even more stunning in this fatigued fairytale than Thomas had ever imagined or remembered. It was as if she was ready for their wedding, with a smile glowing like the stars peeking through the sunset around her. Children were at play, accompanied by small animals all around them, and she was right there, leading each of them.

As the dream came to age, the most beautiful white house and stained wooden porch that wrapped around from the front to the back, appeared. Kawai sat front and center with the same breathtaking smile, ready for storytime with the children and eventual grandchildren. Her skin glistened from the beach to the rocking chair she now sat in, kissed by the most beautiful part of the sun and weathered in the fountain of youth. Kawai appeared to be a mother in the vision that raced through Thomas's sleeping mind, but she had the same youthful smile, never breaking to talk or direct the children that sped by her feet.

With every change of scenery, everything seemed to be perfect. Stacks of letters sat beside Kawai's still rocking chair, on a hand-made, wooden table, with loose tan string holding them together. No dates, signatures, or addresses were visible, but they were most certainly letter's that Thomas was never able to send Kawai. After the final shot and victory parades in this fantasy world, she seemed to finally be able to read them, one by one, hanging onto and cherishing every word.

The woman he loved graced a home that sat on a hill overlooking the most alluring view of the Pacific Ocean. One that Thomas couldn't wait to build and raise a family in. It was his dream to one day tell stories and lessons to his children and grandchildren on a porch like the one pictured in his mind from a simpler time. Nothing compared to a life with the one woman he loved. The woman who swept him off his feet, made him care about another human the way he did his job and gave him something other than rank to fight for. Thomas left his purpose in a frightened sob on the beach of O'ahu, ripped from his arms and thrown into her own war story, one she didn't deserve. For all he knew, a story ended on that beach in cold blood, but one he hoped had an ending like the fairytale that gave him a light in his darkest hour.

Each change in setting brought him closer to Kawai. From the beach, he laid on a blanket, watching her dance and smile in the red and orange sky. On the porch, he sat beside her, watching over the children at play and dogs searching for attention, looking at her face that remained full with the same smile. These events led up to her walking slowly towards Thomas as he stood overlooking the water beneath his dream home, wrapping her arms around him. "This is everything we ever wanted," she said as she leaned in to kiss his cheek. "I'm so glad God brought-"

"Wake up, you spineless coward," a man said, waking Thomas from a deep sleep and dream he wished would have never ended. "You're the only American pig we captured from your squadron, which means more work left for you."

Thomas was still trying to process the dream he had just experienced but was delighted at the news the guard shared with him. It was meant to make him worry or dread what was next, but that's the last thought that crossed his mind. This meant that his mission and goal were accomplished. Every man under his leadership had returned to base with a better chance of going home to their families, safe and sound, with their own futures waiting to become a reality.

The Japanese soldier assigned to push Thomas past his mental and physical limit forced him to his feet and out of the room. Thomas was so focused on the vision he had just experienced that he barely noticed any pain. As the door swung open, his aching feet met wooden walkways built on dirt, surrounded by barbwire fences separating the camp from the jungle that ran as far as Thomas could see.

Thomas was led to a small factory building, where he was put to work on 15-hour shifts with little to no break, assembling equipment for the Japanese War effort. His first day in the steaming factory, with scraps to eat and drink, was the beginning of months of taxing work. Each day brought another American soldier dropping to their knees due to exhaustion, dehydration, or starvation, only to be beaten to a pulp and, in most cases, dying.

Hours were long, work was taxing, and the beatings went straight to the bone. Thomas's weight fell off until only skin protected the ribs that became nearly fully visible from the outside. A clean body and refreshing shower were an afterthought as the days clicked by slower than even the humblest soldier could have predicted. Thomas was a servant for the enemy, left for dead, and not cared even the slightest for. Him nor the men who dropped like flies around him meant anything to the guards who waited impatiently to crack them across the back or throw them into the ground. Holidays came and went without acknowledgment. The weather changed, days grew shorter, then long again, but the work and abuse never wavered.

The necklace that had yet to be found and the fading memory of a dream that gave him hope, even if it was false, pushed Thomas through the fiery hell on all sides of him. Flames of anger and pain grew with every crawling hour, but so did images of Kawai everywhere he turned. With each pause when the Japanese weren't watching, to catch his breath and look into the sky, there she was. Every whisper of the wind held her sweet voice; each cloud formed her smile, and heat from the sun touched Thomas's battered skin gently, just as she did. Splashes of water brought much-needed refreshment and boost of energy to his face, but neither topped the vision of the woman he missed so dearly in the small puddle that formed at the bottom of the worn trough.

Kawai was in every impossible task, dream at night's end and dreadful call to begin when the sun rose. She was with him at every step, through what was left of her hidden necklace and the hope of his fairytale dream of the perfect life. Whether false hope created in his mind, the reason to continue sent from above, or a sign of what was waiting for him, Thomas pushed on because of Kawai and all that made him think about her.

With windy Spring days growing hotter by the second across the prison and inside the factory, Thomas grew weaker. Each beating cut just a bit deeper than the one before and another job less realistic to be finished in a way that satisfied the Japanese guards. America was gaining ground, and the Japanese were throwing a last second hail mary in the most gruesome of manners, directing their pilots to purposely ram their planes into American carriers, looking for any opportunity to kill and advance. Guards found ways to make the experience for POWs even worse as the end of the war neared, hoping to bring as many to their knees as possible. The Japanese were on the ropes, but Thomas struggled to stand toe-to-toe with them, as a summer filled with temperatures to match the landscape of hell were just around the corner.

An extraordinarily hot summer-like sunset beat on Thomas's scarred back. With no crumb of food or sip of water in his body, a man led him back to his cell after his longest shift to date. Thomas couldn't wait to fall into the cool dirt floor. Though muddy from the moisture of the ground beneath him and as hard as the rocks that lined the walls, it was the only relief his body felt all day. The guards were pushing the limits of American bodies and minds, cutting their normal sleep patterns in half and extending their work hours just a bit more with each trip around the clock.

Thomas was beaten to a pulp, exhausted to the point of delusion and the closest to giving up as he had ever been. Kawai and the dream of a life he hoped to experience with her, as long as she was alive and still wanted his presence lived in his mind. Nothing else crossed it; there simply wasn't enough energy to focus on anything else. Lance, his grandparents, Commander Styles, even his squadron, none of that had entered his headspace in months. Kawai's well-being consumed him as he was led back to his cell.

"Is she alive? Does she love me? Did she find someone else to replace me?" Thomas thought as his legs began to give.

"Walk, you coward!" The guard shouted, but Thomas couldn't any longer. He smacked into the ground, tripping over his fatigue and a space between the makeshift wood walkway against his bare and bloody feet.

This was all but an invitation for the men to commence in a beating that would top any Thomas had received up to that point. Punches were thrown to every part of his face, and upper body kicks to the ribs, legs, and head. There was no covering up for protection or attempting to run for safety. Thomas had become a punching bag for two losing men to take the anger of the realities of the Pacific War in mid-1945 out on. Japan was all but finished, and though Thomas didn't know that as he fell unconscious from the continuous blows to the head and chest, all he needed to do was hold on.

Holding on was easier said than done as the guards opened the door to the room Thomas was kept in, working together to throw his unconscious body as hard into the mud wall as possible. His body hit the floor with a gruesome thud, and off they went, locking the door behind them and hoping that was the last breath Lt. Metic would take under their watch.

Thomas's breathless body was battered, but visions of hope refused to leave him alone. Scenes of Kawai dancing under the perfect Hawaiian sun filled his mind. Whether he had died and gone to heaven, with Kawai's angel there to greet him or her beaming smile, a simple sign from God that this wasn't the end of Thomas's road, just the final paragraph of a very painful chapter. Whatever the reason, Thomas wanted to jump into Kawai's outstretched arms and never return to the hell of World War II again.

Many hours passed as Thomas laid in the same position against the blood-stained mud wall behind him. His mind drifted in and out of the same reoccurring vision, and though this was a comfort that had been unmatched before, his body was running out of time. Thomas was suffering from consistent blood loss and internal bleeding from the wounds he suffered at the hands of the Japanese. Remaining unconscious through these painfully long moments, Thomas's only hope was the Japanese coming back to heal him enough to work again or an American troop mustering up the bravery to come looking for him.

On the fifteenth day of May, 1945, the United States Army forces liberated the camp, finding Thomas in dire shape. His body was covered in dirt and torn clothes, with bone that could be seen from a mile away piercing against his starved pale body. Blood stained every particle of clothing, and time wasn't on his side. For many hours, Thomas had been lying, unconscious, in his own blood. Medics raced him to a nearby vehicle, stabilizing him enough to ship him to an awaiting hospital and the care he would need to have a fighting chance at survival.

Thomas was on the mend after several months at various hospitals, taken care of by numerous doctors and nurses. From unconscious days, to slowly understanding what had happened and eventually being able to speak about it, the process was slow and frustrating. With Kawai's battered necklace wrapped around his wrist, Thomas's range of motion and use of each limb came many weeks into his recovery. By a very somber second anniversary of Lance's death, thoughts of home and the war's end had become a very real possibility. It was no longer a hopeful Christmas wish on deaf ears but just a matter of time.

With summer winding down, Thomas began the process of walking, eating, and completing daily tasks without assistance. Next came slow exercise and a few physic evaluations, as plans to return to Hawaii were made.

Hitler had been dead for months, and the war in Europe was over. Celebrations filled the streets of New York, Chicago, and St. Louis, as Americans awaited Victory in Japan and the rest of their men. Thomas was excited, but not in the same way. He was days away from jumping onto a plane, with a new lease on life and the truth about Kawai awaiting him when he touched down.

As Thomas limped aboard the plane that would once and for all take him back to O'ahu, with the warm late-September sun touching his skin, feelings of what could be on the other side of the trip made his healing palms sweat. Nearly four years prior, a similar airliner gave him a third-class ticket to a bout with the mightiest of enemies. One that brought depression, anger, loss, and newfound faith. He was a different man now, someone who had led men through battle, lost his wingman and cheated death many times, but his love for Kawai was stronger than it was then.

Every dream, flashback, and unsent letter brought Kawai closer to him. From her necklace, to the chalk "K.M.," that Thomas never left the carrier without writing, she was with him every step of the way. Somedays, her smile was more vivid in his mind than others, but her memory never left, and the hope that Thomas would one day see that contagious smile, passionate voice, and adorable laugh stayed intact. He had experienced things that no man should have to, but through it all, God made sure Thomas never forgot the last loved one he saw before the war.

Their dreams and goals for the future came and went from his mind but ultimately had stayed with him. Every moment from the two magical nights on the beach, the first time they made love, and how Kawai's smile turned to a frightened cry as he was ripped away from her made Thomas's passion for her grow by the day. Whether it was Kawai's spirit with him at every turn or God using her memory as the strength Thomas needed to fight on and return to her arms, he had survived, and now it was time to find out if she and the love they formed many moons ago, had as well.

With breathtaking O'ahu stars above him, Thomas bypassed all celebrations, ignored the doubt in his mind, and made his way to the Aloha Sun Winery. He was determined to buy two bottles of wine and cover every inch of the island, if necessary, to find the answers to where Kawai may be and what direction her life had taken. Thomas sat down at the longest wood bar he'd ever seen and waited patiently to buy the wine he came for. As he looked down at the worn necklace with two beads on his healing wrist, he saw a glimpse of a person that stopped him in his tracks, made his heart beat faster than any dogfight could, and threw his mind into a time machine.

"Kawai?" Thomas asked quietly, standing slowly from his stool.

"Oh my gosh, it's you," Kawai uttered, as she ran to him.

"I'm sorry, I'm so sorry, sweetheart," Thomas cried as he pulled her close. "I love you, and I'm sorry I never got the chance to tell you. I've thought about this moment every day for years."

"It's really you," Kawai said slowly as she kissed his cheek. "I love you too, and I've never stopped. Every night, I prayed looking into the sunset on the same beaches you held me. I prayed for this moment."

"Are they-" Thomas hesitated, struggling to control his emotion.

"Beth, Kahuna, this is your daddy," Kawai said, putting one arm behind each of their backs.

Every prayer answered, daydream a reality and wish granted. Kawai's hair was shorter, her face slightly aged, but more beautiful than he could ever imagine. Their children, a blessing that never crossed his mind to come home to, were perfect.

Beth had his eyes... Kahuna, his nose. His grandparent's spirit was in each of them, and while he was worrying miles away, they were working their magic here at home. Every loved one they had lost through his short life took care of Kawai, watched over his children, and led Thomas right back to where he was supposed to be.

The warmth Thomas felt as he hugged his family for the first time and kissed Kawai's lips, put him in a state of euphoria. He didn't fully understand it, but it felt right. No matter the horror they had endured, their life was just beginning and though there was no playbook to the mission of family; Thomas knew what to do next, reaching into his pocket to grab Kawai's necklace.

He used his knife to carve "B.M." onto the empty bead, careful to keep the battered necklace with Kawai's initials remaining from countless events, intact. Thomas reached for his dog tags next, leaning down to his son and daughter.

"This is for you, Beth," Thomas uttered, handing the necklace to his daughter. "No matter where your life takes you, this will keep you safe and lead you back home again."

"And Kahuna, I'll tell you about the stories behind these when you're older," Thomas said as he handed his son the dog tags, placing his other arm around Kawai. "Especially those about your uncle Lance."

"I never gave up on you coming back to me," Kawai said with a tear falling down her cheek. "I never gave up on us, all of us and I never will. I love you and what a miracle this is."

"I'm home, you led me home," Thomas whispered calmly, pointing to the stars through a window in the distance. "I love you, all three of you, forever and always."

S.L. Bolin is a historical romance author with a passion for storytelling. *Pacific Hope* is the first of many World War II fictional stories S.L. hopes to bring to light.

Growing up, Bolin's love for the 1940s and the planes that filled its skies became evident at an early age. Films, museums, and novels fueled that passion, and after a brief stint as an auto racing journalist, he set his eyes on the ultimate challenge, writing a novel.

S.L.'s first go at book writing, *The Call*, went unpublished but gave him the experience to put it all together. After two years of working through the idea for Pacific Hope, the novella was born, and confidence for more bloomed.

"I would like to thank my family, friends, and fans, who believed in me enough to reach this point of my first book. I promise always to give my all, bring the stories in my heart to light and never cut corners. The time and money you, the reader, put into consuming my novella are not lost on me, and I will always be thankful for that. This is only the beginning." - S.L. Bolin

To stay up-to-date on future releases, promotions and announcements, visit www.slbolin.com or follow along via Facebook and Instagram (@slbwrites).